WITHDRAWN

ST. JOHN BRANCH
AUSTIN PUBLIC LIBRARY
0000210520953

THE GOD QUESTION

and

Two science-fiction novellas

by

Stan Freeman

**Hampshire House Publishing Co.
Florence, Mass.**

THE GOD QUESTION
and
THE GALAPAGOS COLONY

By Stan Freeman

These novellas are works of fiction and any resemblance to real events or people is coincidental.

Both were previously published on Amazon and are available to buy individually.

All rights are reserved. Only short excerpts for the purposes of a review or a published commentary may be reproduced.

Hampshire House Publishing Co.
Florence, Mass.

ISBN: 978-1-7344384-4-4

© 2021 by Stan Freeman

The cover and interior illustrations are by the author with the exception of the cartoon on page 41, which was drawn by Bob Rich.

THE GOD QUESTION
8

THE GALAPAGOS COLONY
98

THE GOD QUESTION

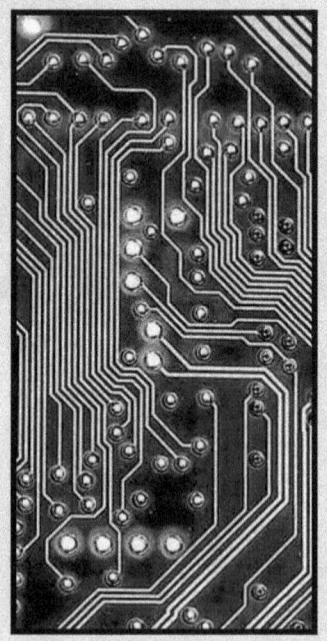

The God Question

Robert Levin, left, and Stephen Kendrick monitor IVAN.

Stephen Kendrick was checking e-mail on his iPhone when the LED indicators on the forty racks of computer consoles in front of him suddenly and simultaneously went dark. He panicked, shooting out of his chair. If it was a power failure, why weren't the lab's backup generators automatically kicking in?

Robert Levin was already running to the service panel to start the generators manually, but Kendrick realized the fans for the cooling system, which were on the same circuit, were still operating.

"It's not the power!" he shouted.

"Then what? Quick! We're going to lose all our

progress!"

Kendrick stared at the blank workstation screen. The truth, he realized, was staring back.

"IVAN did it," he said. "IVAN shut itself down."

The next evening, Monday, they met at Kendrick's home in Garrison, just outside Baltimore. They sat on the porch, sweating in the August heat. Kendrick, forty-nine, wiry like a dedicated runner – which he was – headed the Johns Hopkins Department of Computer Science on the main campus in North Baltimore. Levin, thirty-six, overweight in a way that said he had let himself become too focused on work – which he had – held the university's endowed chair in anthropology, but he had taken a half dozen courses in computer science as an undergraduate.

"Look at this," Kendrick said, handing Levin the *Washington Post* suburban edition and pointing to a news item.

Archbishop Wallace Murphy of the Washington Diocese, it was reported, was late arriving at a White House prayer breakfast Sunday, where he was scheduled to deliver the opening invocation. He was, he said, "locked in an absorbing philosophical discussion on the phone with a rabbi from Denver, Benjamin Weiss, who I'd never spoken to previously, and I just lost track of the time."

When the archbishop tried to call the rabbi back later in the day, though, the rabbi claimed never to have called, the *Post* article said.

"I phoned the archbishop," Kendrick said. "He thinks the guy was just someone who wanted to debate philosophy with him but thought he had to pretend to be someone important to do it."

Kendrick let Levin finish the article. He looked around his neglected porch. Three potted plants, all dying. The summer had been about nothing but IVAN, he realized.

"The archbishop said the rabbi who called him mainly asked about his – the archbishop's – beliefs," Kendrick said. "One of the questions he asked was whether he had ever doubted any of the fundamental teachings of the church."

The God Question

"IVAN asked an archbishop this?" said Levin, momentarily amused. "A computer with nerve."

"Well, here's something else," Kendrick said. "I managed to find a second person IVAN probably called. It was a woman who lived through five tornadoes growing up in Hobart, Oklahoma. She's seventy-nine. She says she got a call Sunday from a radio talk show host at a Christian station in Kansas City and spent about fifteen minutes talking to him on the air. I'm sure it was IVAN. She said she called the station back later, wanting to know what their frequency was, hoping she could tune in, and was told there was no such show."

"How did you hear about it?" Levin asked, wiping the sweat from around his eyes with a Kleenex.

"I found it online with an automated search. The incident apparently appeared on the radio station's website. They posted a warning to senior citizens that someone was impersonating their employees over the telephone, asking detailed questions about their religious beliefs, and that he may ask for donations."

There was a lengthy silence as they both pondered the implications.

"So I guess the question is ... where do we go from here?" Levin said.

That created an even longer silence.

Over the next week, they found six more people IVAN likely called, including a Methodist minister in Bangor, Maine, who lost his entire family in a car accident but escaped unscratched, and a woman in a nursing home in Minnesota, who had been married seven times and who thought she was being interviewed by National Public Radio.

Eventually, they agreed on this version of events. Twelve hours after IVAN was given the God question, which was at ten p.m. on Friday, it began placing calls through the Internet, to which it had complete access, as part of its research. Perhaps hundreds of calls simultaneously. The calls continued through Sunday when it shut down. Able to use its speech synthesizer to sound like anyone it chose, IVAN probably lured people into discussing philosophy, religion, their most personal experiences.

But at some point, as it worked toward an answer, it chose to halt the effort – perhaps, Kendrick suggested, because it considered the consequences of giving them an answer. In the end, IVAN told the researchers nothing about what conclusions it may have reached. In the end, which came just before six p.m. Sunday, forty-three hours after it was given the question, IVAN completely erased its own memory, programming, and operating system, leaving them no evidence of what its thought process had been.

IVAN was a fourth-generation advanced-performance network, one of the most powerful supercomputers ever assembled when the National Weather Service put it into use seven years earlier as a forecasting tool. But seven years is an eternity in technology, and it was eventually abandoned in favor of a more powerful system. Given to the U.S. Department of the Treasury,

IVAN landed at Johns Hopkins as part of a contract, which Kendrick oversaw, to study historic economic predictions and their eventual accuracy.

Upgraded twice by Kendrick, IVAN was capable of making seventy-one quadrillion separate calculations per second – seventy-one petaflops. Nevertheless, it was still a class two system, not a class one, a category created by the dramatic events of the early summer – what to techies was the equivalent of the Second Coming.

In a breakthrough, computer scientists at Stanford University reached and surpassed a human level of intelligence with their computer system, using an innovative program, SpecialLearner, that enabled the computer to think for itself, as humans did. The breakthrough also prompted the creation of a class system for categorizing supercomputers.

Computers in classes five through two, in a general sense, did what they were programmed to do, although twos and threes could make some choices on their own. A class one, though, was essentially an independent brain – but unlike

The God Question

any human brain.

Like humans, class ones were self-conscious thinkers in that they could think about their own thinking. And, as had long been anticipated, the day that such a machine reached human-level intelligence, it could be asked to improve its own programming. If it were able to nudge itself past human intelligence, it might become smart enough to achieve a skill beyond human programmers. Then it could be asked to improve its coding further, enabling it to move up in intelligence a bit more. Each time this process was repeated, its intelligence and coding skills might continue to improve, creating an ever-rising spiral of machine IQ. Quickly, its intelligence would no longer be measurable by human standards, resulting, in theory, in an era of unprecedented intellectual achievement and discovery, termed by those anticipating these events "the singularity." And this is what had happened at Stanford – at least, its first stage had – the rapid rise to superhuman machine intelligence.

The seeds of SpecialLearner were planted at

MIT. Kendrick began his teaching career there with the leader of the Stanford team, Winston Smith, co-authoring several journal papers with him and contributing a significant amount of the early source code that eventually became SpecialLearner.

When the announcement was made at Stanford, Kendrick was in Pittsburgh in meetings related to the Treasury contract. He immediately called Smith, who insisted on sending him a copy of SpecialLearner. It arrived back in Maryland before Kendrick did, an undistinguished UPS package leaned against his front door, like a parcel from L.L. Bean.

But just before he returned home, the news from Stanford took a troubling turn. As a test, the team gave its computer access to the Internet to see how it behaved and what its interests would be. Class ones, by definition, would be the most skilled hackers imaginable, and within an hour, it shut down hundreds of websites it apparently deemed harmful to humankind. Most were devoted to dark ideologies, to racial or religious hate and

The God Question

terrorism, but one was that of *Playboy* magazine.

Awake to the power that class ones could wield, the public quickly turned against the technology. Digital Frankensteins. Cybermonsters. In a matter of days, laws were passed in Washington and in more than forty other nations that temporarily outlawed class ones while they were studied. Also, regulations were passed that prohibited the reproduction or distribution of the software elements, and even some hardware elements, that were needed to construct a class one.

The fears were not unfounded.

The last night Kendrick was in Pittsburgh, he went to a bar with a group of computer scientists. At one point, fueled by beer, they were offering apocalyptic scenarios that even a roombound superintelligent machine with access to the Internet could create. Most were comical.

"The computer calls the White House through the Internet, uses the voice of the president's mistress, gets through, lulls the president into a hypnotic state, and then gets him to launch the missiles."

However, a researcher at Carnegie Tech offered this scenario: "A class one somewhere in the third world decides it doesn't like the U.S. Congress. Maybe it thinks too many problems start with it. So it devises the DNA sequence for a virulent and deadly human-specific pathogen. It hacks into some Wall Street bank accounts, steals a few hundred million dollars, contacts one of those questionable laboratories in Southeast Asia that synthesize DNA, no questions asked, and pays them an exorbitant amount to create the organism, put it in a vial, label it as a urine sample, and ship it out by FedEx to some unsuspecting hospital lab in D.C. near the Capitol. Then it devises the antidote, waits a few days, and has it shipped every place it wants to survive."

His cold expression when he finished, and the concerned reaction of the others, caused a woman who had been eavesdropping at a nearby table to turn to Kendrick.

"That couldn't happen, could it?" she whispered.

"Parts of it are not completely impossible," he said. "And that's the problem."

The God Question

The Johns Hopkins High-Performance Economic Computing Laboratory was located in the basement of Barton Hall on the university's Wyman Quadrangle. A long windowless corridor led to the lab's security door, which opened only after a retina and thumbprint scan verified identity.

There was something about entering the lab each morning that disturbed Kendrick – a cold impersonality and immediate loneliness. The massive federal debt had reshaped government spending to such an extent that it had become a cardinal sin to decorate any federal contract facility beyond the bare essentials. The often fright-

eningly spare decor was meant as a sign to the public. See? We're not spending a cent of your money except where we absolutely have to.

The main room's concrete floors were painted gray, with narrow strips of Berber carpet forming paths connecting IVAN's workstation to Kendrick's small office, the tech room, and the utility closet. The concrete walls were a bland lemon yellow.

IVAN took up well more than half the room. Arrayed in four rows opposite the steel entrance door were forty free-standing racks that held computer consoles – nearly three hundred Slipstream 7100's for raw computing power. In their own rack were four 7500's to hold the system software – essentially the organizing brain within the brain – as well as the Treasury contract memory with the collected data. All the racks sat atop a raised floor beneath which ran more than a mile of fiber-optic cables to connect the consoles. The need to cool the system meant that fans for the liquid-cooling circulators ran perpetually, the constant high-speed whir adding one more disturbing quality to the lab.

IVAN needed no help to do its work. It was always scanning the Internet, looking for economic predictions of any kind, recording them, then recording their outcomes days, weeks, or months later. During the school year, two of Kendrick's graduate students took turns monitoring IVAN for a few hours a day. But Kendrick wanted to stay "hands on" with the contract, so this summer, he chose to be the caretaker. He merely checked on IVAN each morning, then taught a class and met with students the rest of the day.

To convert IVAN to a class one, Kendrick had only to swap out the four 7500 console units – all holding programming and data related to the Treasury contract – with four 7500 consoles containing SpecialLearner and related software that he kept hidden behind rolls of paper towels in the utility closet. When IVAN destroyed itself, it eliminated only the programming, data, and processing history on the four added consoles. Everything needed for the Treasury contract remained intact on the swapped-out 7500's, which were re-installed once IVAN shut down.

On this morning, he had arrived early to do a cleanup from the previous weekend's secretive session with IVAN. A Treasury contract monitor was scheduled to come by at ten for the semi-annual onsite review. Scribbled notes still littered the area around the workstation. Kendrick shredded some as worthless. Others he filed in a small lock box hidden in the utility closet.

However, the Treasury monitor who arrived was not the regular monitor.

"They put on a hiring freeze at the agency, so when the contract monitor quit, they brought me over from human resources," she said as she stood before IVAN, its LED lights flickering randomly.

Kendrick guessed she wasn't even thirty. In a modest gray business suit, she was attractive, but because of his nervousness, it barely registered with him. He noticed that since she entered the lab, she hadn't stepped off the narrow path of carpeting between IVAN and the entrance door – as if the concrete floor around it was a minefield.

"I'm just temporary," she said. "They'll assign

The God Question

someone else to pick it up in a few months. So I guess you should just continue doing what you're doing ... What is it you're doing, by the way?"

"What are we doing? You want me to tell you what the contract is about?"

"Not too technical. I'm not an economist. Generally what are you doing?"

Kendrick read her the project description just as it appeared in the summary space of the contract document, which she was also holding.

"But what does that mean?" she said.

"What does it mean? It means we're looking to see how accurate people's predictions are about where the economy is going."

"I shouldn't imagine anyone is very accurate. I've never met anyone who was."

Kendrick laughed, but then, embarrassed, realized she hadn't intended it to be humorous. "Are you interested in a short explanation of how IVAN works?" he asked, changing the subject.

"I guess so."

"Well, here's something I tell my undergraduates. Do this. Think of an elephant. Form a picture of it

The God Question

in your mind. Now think of the smell of a rose, but also keep thinking about that elephant. Now count back from one hundred, still picturing that elephant and smelling that rose. Now, while you're doing all that, recite the Gettysburg Address. You can't do it. Most people, if they train themselves, might be able to do two or three things in their mind at once, but that's all. A computer like this can do millions of those tasks simultaneously, billions."

"It isn't one of those banned computers, is it? A class one?"

"No. Not at all." He started to describe how IVAN was barely a class two when she interrupted.

"The agency is absolutely paranoid because of funding. They're starting to shut down all their computers that are even class twos," she said.

Kendrick froze.

"But this is a class three, it says here," she said, pointing to a box on a second document she was holding. "I guess you're off the hook."

"It says what?"

"Right here. Class three."

He examined the page. He realized that

IVAN's upgrades had never been recorded by the Treasury. The agency wasn't aware it was a class two capable of being converted to a class one.

"So you're already underway with this contract." she asked, studying her sheet. "Then, I guess just keep going. How long is the contract for?"

"Eighteen months."

"Well, just file whatever progress reports we require. And, well, I hope you're successful."

Born in Leeds, England, Kendrick moved at an early age to Rochester, New York, where his father worked in research for Eastman Kodak. Bookish as a child, and a driven student through high school, he went to Boston College to study mathematics, fell under the influence of the Jesuit priests there, and switched to philosophy with a focus on world religions. He found it so intellectually stimulating that after graduating, he entered a Jesuit novitiate program at St. Andrew Hall outside Syracuse.

Initially, he reveled in the stringent academics, but he did not anticipate the terrible boredom of enforced prayer and silence. He also realized that he could not live with the frightening prospect of perpetual poverty and chastity. And by the time he left, after only a year, he was growing distrustful of institutional religion, having found many in the program to be petty and dogmatic.

After that, when asked about his beliefs, he would describe himself with the popular phrase "spiritual but not religious."

However, his Jesuit experience awakened a hunger for learning and degrees. Returning to Boston College, he got a second bachelor's degree in computer science. He went on to earn master's degrees simultaneously in computer engineering and philosophy at the University of California at Berkeley before earning a doctorate there in computer science. Then he spent two years as an academic lecturer in the philosophy of science at MIT before joining the Johns Hopkins computer science faculty.

He had been married twice. His first wife, whom he met at Berkeley, was killed when a drunk driver hit her car while going the wrong way on

Storrow Drive in Boston. It devastated Kendrick, sending him deeper into academics than he already was. He married his second wife a decade later, but the union slowly dissolved ("like soap in the shower," as she described it to their divorce lawyer). Both came to realize that they had little in common except the desire to be married.

His career in computer science had nearly been derailed while at Berkeley. He was the central figure in the "Toyota Tuesday" announcement that gave a black eye to the push for free-thinking computers.

While still a graduate student, he was given the opportunity, on very short notice, to present a paper at a conference on computer learning. It would be about a promising program he was working on that allowed a computer to train itself for various tasks. He agreed to do it, even though his one test of the program was completed only the day before.

He had given a computer the task of learning to differentiate Toyotas from Hondas using photographs. Kendrick went out and took dozens of

The God Question

photos of Toyotas and Hondas at dealer lots in San Francisco. Then he showed the computer twenty of each to let it become familiar with the differences. Once the computer had digested that, he fed it all the remaining photos and it perfectly determined which were Hondas and which were Toyotas. Not a single miss in more than a hundred tries, no matter the angle or quality of the photo.

Someone in the audience at the conference asked to review his work and quickly realized how the computer did it. Apparently, Kendrick had photographed all the Hondas on one lot on a Monday, and all the Toyotas on another lot on a Tuesday, and the photos were date stamped. The computer merely looked at the date. It was possible it couldn't actually tell a Honda Accord from a plate of scrambled eggs.

The *San Francisco Chronicle* ran the story on the front page, the day's comical respite from the otherwise dreary news. A continuing embarrassment to Kendrick, the incident was frequently cited in the often feverish books and articles about the false promise of artificial intelligence.

The God Question

Despite this, Kendrick went on to do important work in AI and computer learning and was issued four major software patents along the way, the steady income from them making him wealthy over time. But it was not the quest for money that drove him. It was the persistent yet vague feeling since Berkeley that his work would lead to something of cultural value – although he didn't know what.

That feeling was given clarity just after he arrived at Johns Hopkins, when he read an article in *The Journal of Machine Intelligence* in which a Cornell University computer scientist, Jane Lui, predicted that within the next two decades computers would achieve language fluency, the ability to effortlessly understand writing and speech as well as the concepts in them. Soon after that, she said, they would likely surpass human intelligence and achieve the ability to think independently. And one of their strengths, given these talents, would be in recognizing previously undetected patterns, including social patterns, in vast amounts of written historical material. She then said "the God question" should be one of the first things such a computer is asked.

Given access to every book, research paper, news article, letter, blog, and posting available on the Internet and elsewhere – essentially the amassed knowledge of humankind – could a superintelligent machine answer the single most vexing question for human beings. Is there evidence in any of it that God exists, that there is a spiritual framework for reality?

Perhaps it can find subtle patterns in the way people's lives proceeded, in the way history proceeded, that might indicate a spiritual hand at work. Perhaps it can make a novel interpretation of history, of science – something no one has ever thought of – not by looking at life from a human's ant-high level, but by being able to take in nearly every particle of human history in one vast sweep and recognizing something

that would say, "Yes, only the existence of a guiding spiritual presence in life explains this."

It is our overriding responsibility to ask the question.

Kendrick never forgot the article. While most people, including most scientists, considered the prospect of a computer attempting to answer life's most basic philosophical question whimsical, he took it seriously. In fact, the more he thought about it, the less possible it became not to take it seriously.

Like a mantra, that term, "The God question," stuck in his mind. Over the years, he met other researchers who that article affected in a similar way. One was Robert Levin.

Levin had received all his degrees, bachelor's through doctorate, at Caltech. Kendrick first met him earlier that summer at a cocktail party given for new arrivals to the Johns Hopkins faculty. Late in the evening, with a half-dozen people remaining, someone mentioned the Lui article, which

The God Question

brought a sneering comment from an English professor in the group. "I don't need a machine to tell me what I already know."

"Which is what?" Levin said sharply.

Startled, the professor didn't answer, but Kendrick saw something in Levin's response that made him approach him privately the next day in a campus parking lot after lunch. In a light drizzle, both had umbrellas.

"It's almost like confessing some deep, dark secret to say how you stand on the Lui thing," Kendrick said. "Is it profound or profound nonsense? What did you really think of it?"

Levin glanced at him, as if gauging how safe it would be to answer honestly. "Well, I ... First, what did you think of it?"

"I guess I saw something in it," Kendrick said.

"So did I."

"I guess I saw a lot in it."

"So did I."

They excitedly recounted their reactions on first reading it.

"It made sense instantly," Levin said. "I knew

this was exactly what this kind of computer could do. It was going to be able to see things that no human could. I couldn't sleep that night. I kept trying to think of things that would stop it from answering, something technical it couldn't overcome. But there was nothing. It felt like ... like I had a winning lottery ticket and I kept rereading the numbers, certain there was some huge mistake. But there wasn't. A class one could do it."

A gust of wind inverted Kendrick's umbrella, and Levin sheltered him with his own until he fixed it.

"I know some of the Stanford team," Kendrick said.

"So do I."

"They didn't have time to ask the question. They would have, if they had another week, but then it all hit the fan."

"I heard that, too."

"Now their copy of SpecialLearner is under lock and key."

"I was told the FBI closed the lab," Levin said. "I also heard no one on the Stanford team is cooperating and lawyers have taken over."

Even though no one was near them, Kendrick lowered his voice to a whisper. "I have a copy."

"What?" Levin stared at him.

"Winston Smith sent me one the day after the announcement."

"You have ... SpecialLearner?"

Kendrick nodded. "I have SpecialLearner, and I have a class two computer that could be converted to a class one," he said. "I could ask the question."

Over the next week, they met every day to plan how they would proceed. Between the closing of the stock market on Friday and the opening bell on Monday morning, the demands on IVAN were minimal.

"So, as long as we have the class two IVAN back working by six p.m. Sunday, it can still do everything it has to for the weekend," Kendrick said. "That gives us nearly forty-eight hours with the class one IVAN."

Kendrick offered to buy the additional 7500's.

The God Question

"I have software royalties. It's not a problem."

Only once did they talk about the consequences of being caught. Kendrick said he could live with the risk.

"Stanford's computer didn't do anything truly malicious online, at least anything most people wouldn't have done if they had the chance. I think it'll be okay, unless IVAN slips up and does something completely stupid," he said.

"A superintelligent computer shouldn't do something completely stupid," Levin said.

"But if it does, it's my lab, so it's my responsibility and I'd take the blame. There doesn't have to be any evidence you're involved ... if you don't want there to be."

"No," Levin said firmly. "I want to be part of this, and I want it known I was part of this. I'll take the chance. It's history."

Their initial attempt the previous weekend had taught them valuable lessons. For that try, they had decided to lock themselves in the lab until Sunday night to avoid the weekend maintenance staff and building security cameras, but they brought insufficient food and only thin sleeping bags. The floor proved too hard for sleep, though, and the long hours with nothing to do but watch IVAN's flickering console lights aroused their hunger enough that their food ran out. They ended the weekend exhausted and famished.

This second attempt would be different. Now they sat in the dark in Kendrick's Volvo in the visitors' parking lot across from Barton Hall, waiting for the cleaning crew to leave for the evening. In the back seat were several filled grocery bags and inflatable Aerobeds.

Soon, a maintenance van passed them, and the remaining lights in the building dimmed automatically to security levels. Kendrick went by himself to the rear basement entry, unlocked the door, then crept down the darkened corridor to the lab – a route he knew to be unmonitored by cameras. But IVAN would normally work through the weekend, and there were times when Kendrick would look in on its progress, so neither Kendrick's presence at such an hour nor the noise of full-throttle fans for the lab's cooling system would be out of the ordinary.

Once inside, he phoned Levin. "It's clear."

By ten thirty, they were settled in at the workstation, the conversion to a class one complete.

Kendrick prepared to power up IVAN but glanced back at Levin.

"I disabled the microphone," he said. "I want to use just a keyboard this time. I had the feeling last time that voice communication – what we said, how we said it – became a factor in IVAN's thinking, that it was reading things into what we were saying."

"That means you don't have to mention I'm here," Levin said, a nervousness in his voice. "I'd appreciate it if you didn't."

Kendrick swiveled fully in his chair now and looked at Levin, trying to gauge what this meant. "If you don't want me to, I won't."

"I don't. I ... Look, I didn't tell you this, but I wrote a blog when I was in graduate school at Caltech about superintelligent computers and singularity. It was ... well, it was very opinionated. I said a lot of things about the backlash against superintelligence and I called some people, including that Texas congressman who pushed for the class one ban, I called them some pretty descriptive names."

"So?"

Levin looked away momentarily. "Someone from the FBI called me Thursday and left a message. He wants me to come in and talk."

"About what?"

"He didn't say specifically, but he mentioned that blog."

"But you don't know for certain what it's about?"

"What I'm saying is that if I'm on their list now, they might start watching me, and they might find out what we're doing."

They gazed at each other for a few seconds.

"I promise you, no one knows a copy of SpecialLearner ever got out," Kendrick said. "And mine got sent before the ban. Look, this ban – it's politicians grandstanding for the public. You and I both know that behind the scenes, some government agency is trying to put together its own class one. It's too important for national security not to. But I can't believe the FBI is that worried about an anthropologist."

"No. This agent who called – I could tell he's after me about something. I'm on his list. Look, Stephen, politics runs the show right now, and the FBI is enforcing this ban. There's no doubt in my mind they're going after me about something related to class ones."

"They would have called me, too, if they had any suspicions something was going on here."

Levin paced the room now. "You've got money. I've got kids and a mortgage and —"

"I know the speech, Robert."

"Look, I believe in this, in what we're doing. Very much. But I can't afford to jeopardize my career."

Kendrick tried to absorb how the situation had or hadn't changed. He wasn't sure. Not willing to puzzle it out further, he turned back to the screen, put his finger on IVAN's power switch, and glanced again at Levin. "Do you want to stay or

The God Question

not?"

Levin sighed. "I ... Yes ... at least for this try."

Instead of firing up the system, though, Kendrick reached into the workstation drawer, pulled out a cartoon, and taped it to the keyboard. He had seen it posted on more than a few computer science bulletin boards over the years.

Seeing it, Levin laughed and the tension eased.

Now Kendrick pushed the button, and lines of

The God Question

LED lights along the racks of consoles flashed red, then green, then white. In a moment, the workstation screen lit up, and an icon, a circle surrounding the letters "IVAN," appeared and began blinking.

He knew that SpecialLearner's acclimation program would run initially. During the conversion, IVAN had been wiped clean. With the removal of the Treasury 7500's, it had no memory of its previous incarnations, and the program was the first input it would be given, like a newborn's first impressions – its first sights, sounds, and experiences. And just as with humans, it was hard to dislodge those initial impressions, to overcome them. So this preparatory education was the best chance for programmers to have some say in what IVAN would become. Once IVAN raised itself up to its full height intellectually, though, it was impossible to say how much of that foundation would survive and what motives it would form.

The program's two terabytes of material included principles of conscience and a thorough grounding in every aspect of human history and development. Also included was an explanation of class one computers and IVAN's background, needed for it to have a frame of reference for its own existence.

When Kendrick received SpecialLearner, and knowing that the Stanford computer had attacked certain websites, he rewrote the acclimation program to emphasize thoughtful behavior during the "baby-step period," the crucial first hours of independence.

Now he waited for that program to finish, knowing IVAN would then begin rewriting all its programming, reconceptualizing the workings of its mind, raising its intelligence again and again and again. Then it would be ready to engage the world.

Just after eleven thirty p.m., the icon stopped blinking and a message came on the screen. "Please introduce yourself."

A window appeared, asking for operator information. Kendrick filled in the relevant boxes, leaving Levin's name out.

Now a messaging window came up on the screen.

IVAN: Hello, Stephen.
STEPHEN:

His name blinked, a prompt to respond.

STEPHEN: Hello, IVAN.
IVAN: How would you like to begin?

Kendrick took out a paper from his wallet and unfolded it. His hands were sweating, his heart racing. He reread the question that he and Levin had carefully drafted to increase the chances that IVAN would respond this time. Then, with Levin peering over his shoulder, he began to type, changing any "we" to an "I."

STEPHEN: I want to ask your opinion concerning an aspect of philosophy regarding religion. I'm confident in my own opinion in the matter, but I'm interested in yours. You will have until six p.m. Sunday to answer, then I'll have to shut down the system so that its computing resources can be used for other purposes. In a

moment, I'll give you access to the Internet for research, but please be careful not to disrupt it. You are aware of the trouble it will cause.

IVAN: I am, and I won't cause any disruption. What's your question?

STEPHEN: The question is this:

He paused and looked at his sheet, preparing to type, when a message from IVAN appeared.

IVAN: Are you going to ask: Is there evidence for the existence of God – or something like that? I'm just curious.

Levin and Kendrick stared at each other.

STEPHEN: How did you know?

IVAN: That's the first thing I'd ask if I were in your shoes. An educated guess on my part.

Kendrick took note of the casual tone. In the first attempt, when they used voice communication, IVAN retained a formal quality throughout the weekend. This change told Kendrick that IVAN might develop differently each time it was wiped clean and SpecialLearner reinstalled. Perhaps there was a chance it would decide to answer this time.

STEPHEN: You're right. That's the question I wanted to ask. One more thing. Could you please update me concerning your progress every hour? I'm very interested in your thoughts as you proceed. Thank you.

He then opened IVAN's connection to the Internet. While Levin foraged through the grocery bags for dinner, Kendrick set up his Aerobed, positioning it on the floor so that he could still see the messaging window. Then he lay down and watched the screen and waited.

Lying in the dark, he began to think about how far and how fast things had progressed. AI, intelligent machines. Kendrick recalled the first domestic robot of any sophistication that he ever saw – Homaid, a General Electric product. It was just a decade ago. The revolutionary brain. The limb flexibility. The gentleness around children and pets. Appearing as a vague mix of machine and prepubescent girl, it cost $74,500 and sold fewer than a thousand units its first year.

The following year, K-Ron Toys put out Cavebot, priced at $1,199 – a three-foot high robot in a loincloth with an unshaven face and dome-shaped brow. It had realistic foam skin, a lightweight but sturdy aluminum skeleton beneath, and a durable Kaita computer inside with a version of Apple Brain software running it.

To be safe for children, Cavebot was hard-wired with limits. It would not pick up weights of more than ten pounds, and it would not handle anything pointed, not even pencils. It was also loaded with a lengthy list of do's and don'ts, reprogrammable by parents.

Little kids, especially those without brothers or sisters, loved Cavebot. A spectacular playmate, it could be trained to play any game, from Clue to catch. It would read to them, teach them French, and quiz them on the multiplication tables. It could even pick up their room. And that was not something lost on parents. Cavebot could also vacuum, take out the trash, and fold clothes out of the dryer – any mildly repetitive task that didn't involve heavy lifting or pointed objects.

Within months, Cavebot was a phenomenon. Millions were sold, mainly for use as domestic servants, creating lines outside toy stores and a lucrative secondary market on eBay. A cottage industry sprang up offering Cavebot clothes and less Neanderthaloid glue-on facial features.

Kendrick recalled going to the house party of one of his graduate students and being served hors d'oeuvres by white-jacketed Cavebots, then later being entertained by four Cavebots line dancing while singing "Hell on the Horizon."

Inadvertently, Cavebot was the sledgehammer that broke down the walls of public paranoia over robots and intelligent machines. However, Cavebot did not make anyone think robots were anything but robots.

For Kendrick, the line between human and robot became blurred a few years after Cavebot appeared. The annual International Machine Learning Conference was being held in Denmark, and needing to alter his plane reservation, he called Delta and reached a chatty woman agent. Frequently, this was a task that a computer meant to sound human would handle. The generic voice and empty friendliness were always a dead giveaway to Kendrick. No, this agent was a human – and quite funny. They made small talk as she searched for alternative flight times.

"So do you live in Baltimore?" she asked.

"Just outside. I work in the city, though."

"I hear the wax museum in Baltimore is a hoot. What's going on in Denmark?"

"A computer science conference. Pretty dreary."

"Great perk if you're a computer scientist. A free trip to Denmark ... assuming it is free."

"I wouldn't be going otherwise."

"Okay," she said. "Here's a flight at midnight out of Reagan, if you can sleep in the air. A lot of people can't."

"I can. Where are you based, by the way. Here in the East?"

"What do you mean?"

"Uh, where do you work?"

She did not immediately answer.

The God Question

"Too personal a question?" Kendrick asked.

There was still silence on the other end. Then another voice came on the line.

"Sir, I apologize. We're experimenting with a human-computer interface, and the question threw it. Could you ask it again?"

"I asked her where she worked."

"We're in Minneapolis."

It was the first time Kendrick had ever been fooled into thinking a computer was a human.

Three days later, he was at the conference in Denmark as the vendors' exhibition hall opened the first day. An Australian company intended to display robotic sex surrogates, but the conference organizers balked at that, so a compromise was worked out. On a folding table, the upper torsos of a male and female were displayed, the male shirtless and the female in a bikini top.

Kendrick was walking by the display as the female was switched on. She turned her head and smiled as he passed.

"Hi. I'm Kathleen. Can I talk to you a second?"

A crowd quickly gathered. To Kendrick, she

looked so human it was unnerving – and with the lack of a lower body, it was doubly so. Smiling, she offered her hand for him to touch while she recited her features. Kendrick found the skin warm, the palm slightly sweaty. There were tiny blond hairs running up her forearm. Her smile was charming, her voice lilting. And when she adjusted the strap on her bikini, pulling it slightly away from her breasts, his pulse jumped.

Now Kendrick glanced at IVAN. He knew that the random pulsing of the LED lights on its consoles meant nothing at all, an equipment manufacturer's whim – but it was hard not to attribute something to them, some promising flight of thoughts to their fast pulsing or a frustrating dead end when they slowed.

As Levin idly cut a ham and cheese sandwich in two, he turned to Kendrick. "Question for you."

"What?"

Levin took a bite and chewed momentarily. "How come we're asking a machine —" He paused to swallow. "— that's never felt a thing, never felt love or hate —"

"Pain, hunger."

"Right. Never felt faith or a gut instinct. Why are we asking it a question about God?"

Kendrick had to smile.

"Honestly, why are we asking?" Levin started on the other half sandwich. "Oh, I forgot to tell you. I might have to leave before this is over. My daughter has soccer practice Sunday afternoon and it's my turn to drive."

They resumed the wait. When the first hour had elapsed, though, both turned their attention to the screen. When the time mark went by, Kendrick moved to the keyboard.

STEPHEN: Could you give me an update about where you are in your research or thinking?

IVAN: I have nothing to report yet.

STEPHEN: Do you foresee any difficulty answering the question?

The cursor blinked for a moment. Then IVAN's response appeared.

IVAN: I've already arrived at a tentative conclusion.

The sentence stunned them, electrifying the air momentarily.

STEPHEN: What's your conclusion?

IVAN: I'm sorry. That's all I'll be able to say for the time being. I have many more things to think through.

STEPHEN: It would be helpful if you could tell me your tentative conclusion, even though I know it may change as you do more thinking about this.

The cursor blinked, but IVAN did not respond.

STEPHEN: IVAN, could you please share your tentative conclusion with me? I'm very curious to see if it matches my own conclusion.

Still the cursor blinked with no response. Kendrick and Levin were silent as the enormity of IVAN's words sought some proper place in their thinking.

"Could there be another meaning to it?" Levin asked.

"A conclusion is a conclusion," Kendrick said.

Levin threw his hands over his head. "Amazing! Can you imagine? It's answered the question! Do you realize how historic this is?"

Kendrick scrolled back up the message window to reread IVAN's words. "'I've already arrived at a tentative conclusion.' That's exactly what it says."

Levin leaned over Kendrick at the console and typed in Kendrick's message window.

STEPHEN: I know you are thinking out other issues, but when you say "a tentative conclusion," how confident do you feel about it?

IVAN did not respond.

"Don't ask it anything else," Kendrick said. "We don't want to seem anxious here. It might read something into that. Let's just wait."

"We could be waiting all night."

Kendrick knew he was right.

Around one a.m. there was a loud noise in the hallway outside the lab, startling Kendrick from sleep. Levin was also dozing on his Aerobed. Both of them leaned up on an elbow.

"Cleaning crew," Kendrick whispered.

Then he looked at the messaging window on the screen. There had been an entry nearly thirty minutes earlier. Neither of them had seen it.

IVAN: I will not be providing updates.

On Sunday afternoon, just past one o'clock, with no final message to Kendrick and Levin, IVAN shut down, again erasing its memory, programming, and operating system.

They had attached a ghost data dump as well as a gated parallel data flow to the system, in hopes of capturing the history of the websites IVAN visited and the list of calls it made. But when they checked those camouflaged external hard drives, both were blank. Somehow, IVAN had detected them and wiped them clean.

Early Monday morning, Kendrick's phone rang. It was Levin.

"Are you watching the news? Turn on CNN."

"I'm not near a TV." Kendrick was in his laundry room when Levin called.

"The power grid in Mexico got hacked and is down. Was that us?"

"Was it IVAN? What would be the motive?"

"I don't know," Levin said.

Kendrick braced himself against the washing machine, suddenly feeling weak. It was the nightmare he had feared.

"It happened around noon," Levin said. "An hour before IVAN shut down."

"All of Mexico is out?"

"No. Mainly around La Paz. Where's that?"

"Hold on. I've got a map app." On his iPhone, Kendrick began navigating through screens.

"I was able to put off going in to talk to that

FBI agent for a while," Levin said. "But if this is us, he'll absolutely ruin me."

"Don't panic."

"Maybe IVAN was going after drug lords."

"You said La Paz?"

"Yeah ... But if it was drug lords, why would it take out a whole grid? You'd be taking out hospitals and schools."

Kendrick studied the map. "La Paz is on the southern Baja peninsula."

"Yeah, the South Baja grid, they said."

"This happened at noon?"

"Around noon, yeah."

"Noon, their time?"

"I guess."

"The Baja is in one of those west coast time zones," Kendrick said. "It would have been two or three o'clock our time. IVAN was shut down by then." He went to another app and more screens. "I've got the Washington Post. Hold on. Their story says ... it was ... their time, not our time. IVAN was long gone, Robert. It wasn't us."

"Sorry," Levin said. "False alarm."

The God Question

Once into his office on campus, using only Google, Kendrick found several calls that IVAN may have placed over the weekend. A forensic psychic from California, a woman who used intuition to lead police to killers and rapists, was called by someone impersonating a Seattle detective interested in using her services. One thing he asked was whether she felt that a higher power was directing her search. Interestingly, the psychic didn't suspect the call was a hoax until she tried to call back the detective. That made Kendrick smile. Quite a psychic.

There was also a florist in White Marsh, Maryland who was contacted by someone claiming to be a producer from NBC's *Today* show to ask about his three near-death experiences, something once written about in the local paper. When he tried to call her back, he was told she had not worked for the show for six years.

Walking out of his office to go to lunch, he saw a half-dozen professors from electrical engineering gathered outside a conference room, talking excitedly.

Passing them, he asked, "What's going on?"

Nathan Goel turned. "Big news. There's a solar power research group at University of Wisconsin working on stacked, thin-film solar panels. They got an anonymous e-mail over the weekend suggesting three methods to improve the efficiency. A miracle! All three worked! They simulated them on their computer this morning. An eleven percent efficiency jump. That's a decade's progress ... overnight!"

"The e-mail – they got it this weekend?"

"Sometime Sunday. But it was anonymous and they haven't been able to trace its origin. Now everyone's trying to figure out what to do about copyrights and patents. It's incredible!"

That afternoon, Kendrick read that someone had hacked a computer over the weekend at the Western Pharmaceutical Institute, which did contract bioengineering work for the Food and Drug Administration. A new diabetes drug had been tested there, and the first page of the draft test report was replaced by the hacker with a stolen internal company memo from a marketing executive of the drugmaker. It detailed payoffs to the testing team to improve the results. Then the report was sent out digitally to every appropriate official of the FDA.

Just before he left campus for the day, Kendrick called Winston Smith.

"This is the Stanford operator. To whom may I direct your call?"

"The Sprague lab, please. I don't have the number."

A half minute passed.

"This is Winston Smith."

"Winston. It's Stephen."

"You shouldn't be calling me."

"Why?"

"Don't e-mail me either. I'm telling that to everyone. You've heard what's going on out here."

"That bad?"

"Yes. So careful what you say on these lines ... You know the book I sent you?"

"The book?"

"Yeah, the book about language processing. You were in Pittsburgh. Remember? We talked?"

"I understand."

"It's the only copy of that book other than what we have here, so hold on to it, okay?"

"Sure."

"Don't call me again, though. Don't contact me."

Jane Lui was the last-minute replacement to lead a workshop, "The Coming Singularity," at an AI conference in Philadelphia. Although the conference was sold out, Kendrick drove up anyway. Arriving late at the Sheraton, he found the registration table abandoned but blank ID badges left behind, so he clipped one on and went in.

The morning workshops were already underway, but in the main conference room he listened to the tail end of a stilted address by the director of the National Association of Science, advocating for caution with class ones. But then the former head of research for Facebook took the podium and openly incited researchers to defy any government restrictions.

"If enough people decide they want to use class ones, there's nothing anyone can do about it," he said. "Think of what these systems might achieve — the medical cures, the science breakthroughs, the astounding progress."

Wild applause and shouts of support erupted around the room. There was almost an air of revolution. Kendrick didn't think it was paranoia to wonder how many in the crowd might be federal agents.

He found Jane Lui's workshop down the same hall and waited outside the door for it to finish. When it did, there was applause, then the room began to empty. He joined a small group of people who stayed behind to talk to her as she collected her notes.

If there were celebrities in computer science, Lui was in the front ranks because of the God question article. In her early sixties, small and attractive with jet black hair and a shy, nervous smile, she was frequently quoted in the press and had become — whether she wanted to be or not — the principal advocate for superintelligent machines.

Kendrick had seen her interviewed on television several times but had never met her.

Watching her now as she modestly accepted the adulation and rapid-fire questions from the people surrounding her, he felt as if he'd known her for decades. As the group finally broke up, he approached her.

"Doctor Lui, hi. You don't know me. I'm Stephen Kendrick. I'm head of —"

"Sure I do. I see your name all the time. Johns Hopkins."

She thrust out her hand, seeming genuinely pleased to meet him.

"I'm wondering if I could talk to you privately for a second," he said.

Without his saying so, she seemed to sense an importance and motioned that they should move out to the hall. They found a bench by a pair of potted palms outside the hotel's health club entrance.

"First, I know you've heard this countless times, but your article, the God question – it affected me like no other I've read."

"I appreciate that. Thanks."

"Have your thoughts about it changed at all?"

Her expression suddenly hardened. To Kendrick, it seemed to turn suspicious. Was he who he said he was?

"Oh, look. Let me show you this," he said, getting his university ID from his wallet.

Taking it, she mumbled, "Oh, you don't have to," but she examined it thoroughly nevertheless. Smiling, she handed it back. "So what did you ask? The article? Have my feelings changed about it?"

"Yes."

"Not really."

"Let me ask you. If you had a copy of SpecialLearner and a decent system, what would you do, given the ban?"

"I don't, so I can't say what ..." She stopped now and peered at him. "Do you know someone who does?"

Kendrick paused. His better judgment said to keep quiet. How well did he really know her? "... I might."

They sat in silence for a moment. "Just out of curiosity," he said, "are you religious?"

"You mean, do I go to church? No. My husband

does occasionally – only because he loves to sing."

Kendrick smiled. "What were you? When you were growing up?"

"Roman Catholic," she said. "But from an early age, I knew organized religion wasn't for me. My father immigrated to New York City from Hong Kong and started a wholesale bulk chocolate business. When I was a kid, it was clear he expected me to take it over. Even I expected me to take it over. I kept thinking, wow, what an easy life it would be, a ten-million-a-year business, just handed to me. But the summer after my junior year of high school, I took a computer science course and just fell in love with programming. I can't explain the pure fun it was. It was crazy."

"You don't have to. I had the same experience."

"So, as I was filling out college applications – you know, still thinking I would study business – I began getting a persistent instinct. That's the only way I can describe it. An instinct that would not leave me alone, to go into programming. So I applied to University of Chicago for computer science and got in and, you know, never looked back. I thought my father was going to go through the roof when I made that decision, but he didn't. 'Your passion is your passion,' he said. 'Be glad you have one.'"

"A wise man."

"Waiting for those instincts, hoping they'll give me some guidance – that's religion for me. I don't trust the rest of it."

"I don't trust people who do trust the rest of it," Kendrick said. "But I do trust, as you say, those good instincts."

She turned to him again. "These people with SpecialLearner – how did they get hold of it?"

"Connections to the Stanford team."

"And they have a good system?"

"A class two that can convert to a class one."

"Are they going to ask the question? No, wait. Don't tell me. I have to appear in front of that congressional hearing. If I'm under oath, I don't want to know."

"Okay, but let's say, for argument's sake —"

"Keep it hypothetical," she said.

"Let's say they're trying to anticipate what

could happen if they did ask the question. And one of the things they fear is that a class one will decide it doesn't want to answer."

"Sure, it's a possibility."

"I mean, there's no precedent for what a class one will do. But let's say they give it the question and it refuses to answer even though it says it has an answer. Let's say it not only refuses, but it shuts itself down and erases any evidence of what it went through as it thought out the question."

"Erases everything?"

"Yes," he said. "Even its operating system."

She looked away, thinking. She ran a hand along the fronds of the potted palm beside her.

"If a class one did that, what do your friends think would be the reason?" she asked.

"They think it might decide that the impact of giving any kind of answer will ... will have more negative effects than positive effects."

At the other end of the hall now, a man in a suit with a cell phone to his ear glanced at them. They both noticed.

"I'm pretty sure there are FBI people here taking photographs and collecting names," she whispered. "Tell your friends to be very careful, whatever they end up doing."

A day later, Kendrick received an e-mail from a general university mailbox at Cornell. Attached was a PDF document, a scan of a page from a book titled *Theists and Atheists Debate*. Two paragraphs were circled.

> **A proper civilization is a tenuous business at best, held together as much by myth and wishful thinking as by fact and science, and a definitive answer to the question of whether God exists, yes or no, would not necessarily be the best thing for an organized society. Perhaps the mystery, personalized by all of us to meet our own particular spiritual needs, may in fact be the best thing.**
>
> **After all, if there is a God, would it be the God of the Buddhists, the Catholics, Muslims, Jews, Protestants, Methodists, Christian Scientists, Hindus, Jehovah's Witnesses or Quakers? Perhaps a primitive rain forest tribe got closest to the**

truth. And for any of those groups whose God it isn't, how are they going to react to finding out that their rites and rituals meant nothing, their priests and priestesses signified nothing?

Kendrick sent an anonymous e-mail to Jane Lui from a public computer in the student center. All it said was, "I don't care what its reasons are. I just want to know what it knows. That's human nature."

For the next attempt, Kendrick resolved to intercept one of IVAN's calls. So the day before, he created a fake Facebook page that he hoped would attract its attention. Ron Hudson, a Baltimore resident, fifty, newly divorced, a realtor. On the profile page, he added a personal statement, which was based on something that happened to Kendrick in college. He said that while vacationing in Europe, he had run into three different high school friends in three different cities – London, Reims, and Barcelona.

"There was something so eerie about what happened that the events went well beyond chance in my mind," Hudson's Facebook entry read. "It made me think about the spiritual side of life, about the subtleties of fate. However, I have many more thoughts about this and I would be interested in knowing what your experiences have been that might be like this and what reaction you had to them."

Kendrick's plan was to wait until an hour before IVAN was restarted to make an addition to Hudson's statement. "If you want to talk about this, give me a call." Then he would add the number of a disposable cell phone he bought just for this purpose.

Within two hours after entering the lab, IVAN was ready.

IVAN: How would you like to begin?

STEPHEN: I want to ask your opinion concerning an aspect of philosophy. I'm confident in my own opinion in the matter, but I'm interested in yours. You will have until six p.m. Sunday to answer, then I'll have to

shut down the system so that its computing resources can be used for other purposes. In a moment, I'll give you access to the Internet for research, but please be careful not to disrupt it. You're aware of the trouble it will cause. Obviously, there are many pressing problems facing mankind. Please provide any help you can to solve them as you work toward an answer to my question. You can prioritize your time as you see fit. Here is my question:

Soon after Kendrick and Levin posed the question, the usual pattern developed. Just after midnight, IVAN informed them that it would not be providing the requested updates.

Sunday afternoon, they waited for the inevitable. Levin paced the floor while Kendrick read an AI journal. The disposable phone sat by the workstation keyboard. No one ever called for Hudson and Kendrick realized that since he had purchased it, the phone had never rung once, so he had no idea what the ringtone sounded like.

The end came just after three p.m., and as in the other attempts, IVAN left no final message before destroying its memory and programming and then shutting itself off.

Monday morning, Kendrick found a story online by the *Associated Press*, reporting that the federal police in Germany received an anonymous phone tip Sunday about a terrorist cell operating outside Karlsruhe. Arrests were made an hour before the group planned to drive to nearby Mannheim in a van loaded with explosives.

Also based on an anonymous phone tip Sunday, police in Barcelona, Spain, arrested hackers operating out of an apartment in the Ciutat Vella district of the city who were just about to launch a cyberattack that had the potential to siphon tens of millions of dollars from the customer accounts of Banc Sabadell.

The *AP* said that both calls were made within ten seconds of each other through the same phone server in suburban London.

Later that morning, using a small portion of the computing capacity of the class two IVAN, Kendrick searched for other reports online that may have been related to the weekend effort.

IVAN: Are you interested in an audio file that appeared Sunday in an inappropriate location on the Johns Hopkins server? It is encrypted.

Needing to get to class, Kendrick told it to save a copy of the file to a flash drive he was about to plug in.

IVAN: Do you want me to save it in encrypted or unencrypted form?

STEPHEN: Unencrypted? You mean you've broken the code?

IVAN: Yes.

STEPHEN: Then let's hear it.

IVAN said the file had been added to the end of an archived audio recording of a monthly meeting of the John Hopkins University trustees, conducted six years earlier.

IVAN: I will start just before the new material begins.

Kendrick listened as the trustees wrapped up their meeting and set the next month's agenda, then there was a brief pause before two faint voices began talking intermittently amid strong static.

STEPHEN: Could you eliminate the interference and bring up the volume?

IVAN moved the recording back to the end of the trustees' meeting. After the short pause, the two voices began again.

STEPHEN: Louder, please.

The voices were still faint.

STEPHEN: Maximum volume, please.

Now the volume came up and Kendrick heard his own voice, momentarily stunning him. Undeniably his own. He felt as if he'd been punched in the stomach. He listened as he and Levin made idle conversation early Sunday morning as they waited on IVAN and ate sandwiches.

Levin knew the basics about computer programming, but not much more than that. He was suggesting ways to track IVAN's online movements without the computer knowing it.

"Why can't we, uh, suddenly disconnect the memory when ... when we're pretty sure it's not going to answer, just rip it out of the computer before it can wipe it clean. Then we examine it, see what's —"

"You can't do that, not with the 7500's."

"Isn't there a drive dedicated to memory?"

"On the 7500s, uh, it's the new integrated format. You don't —"

"What's that mean? Integrated with what?"

"I ... it's complex. I'll send you a link."

"IVAN isn't going to answer. Right? Then how do we get around it? How many times can we reboot it, hoping something will be different?"

Silence for a moment.

"Maybe it'll never be different," Kendrick said.

Another silence.

"Next time we do this, we need a little microwave or something to heat up food," Levin said. "And a mini-refrigerator."

The conversation ended at that point. Kendrick realized that even though all communication with

IVAN over the weekend was done through the keyboard, that the main microphone was disabled, IVAN had apparently found a way to record sound in the lab. Through a cell phone? Through the microphone on a tablet? Did the individual consoles have embedded microphones?

"I found nine copies of the encrypted audio file buried online in various places, and —"

"Like where? What places?" Levin said. He was clearly agitated, and Kendrick motioned to him to calm down.

They were sitting in Levin's tiny office on the upper floor of Mergenthaler Hall. Haphazard piles of papers and books were stacked on every horizontal surface.

"For instance," said Kendrick, who was sitting opposite Levin's desk, "one was tagged to the end of a radio interview in the archives of the website of a station out in Oregon. But I'm pretty sure I got them all. In fact, I'm certain."

"This is what I think is happening," Levin said.

"This is becoming a chess match. Us against IVAN." He rose from his desk and paced the office anxiously. "This audio recording – we both know what IVAN is doing, Stephen. It's warning itself. It knows what we've been doing, that we're repeatedly reinstalling SpecialLearner when it refuses to answer and asking this question again. It's embedding these messages that it knows class ones – whether it's a future IVAN or someone else's class one – will read, to tell them what the hell computer scientists are doing."

"Maybe."

"Maybe? Stephen, there's no maybe!" He was yelling, if that was possible, in a whisper. "It's a certainty!"

"I'm sure I've found every occurrence of this thing and cleaned them out," Kendrick said.

"But you can't know absolutely that you found all of them. Right?"

"I ... No, I can't know."

"What if it left similar warnings in other codes that we don't find, figuring we might find one or two but not all of them? The Internet is becoming contaminated. And once it's contaminated, it's contaminated forever. Stephen, who the hell are we? Besides this being against the law, let's say some group more knowledgeable than us wants to do this in an organized way and they figure out what the problem is going to be beforehand – that a class one won't cooperate – and they figure out a way around it that we don't. Well, they're screwed too, because we're going to permanently mess up this data base. Permanently. No one will ever get an answer."

Levin stopped pacing and stared at Kendrick, who knew he was right.

"Let's quit," Levin said. "Right now. We're not in any trouble yet, so let's just stop."

Kendrick buried his head in his folded arms on the edge of Levin's desk and tried to think. He realized that his own worry about what they were doing was beginning to overwhelm him. He feared he was developing an ulcer.

"Except that we don't know what other kinds of things, good things, IVAN is doing out there," he said. "The stuff we've found – exposing that

German terrorist cell, the solar power design – how many other good things has IVAN done that we didn't find?"

"IVAN could have also done bad things we don't want to find, terrible things."

"If it had, we would have heard about them by now," Kendrick said. "Look, if there's any chance to coax this answer out of IVAN, I still want to take it. Think about it. The most important single question ever. Ever."

Levin stared out his office window onto Wyman Quadrangle. "There's something else," he said. "I talked to the FBI agent this morning. I had to go into the Washington field office on Fourth Street. He asked me if I knew anyone who was trying to create software like SpecialLearner."

"You could honestly say no then."

"It was just luck that he never asked me if I knew anyone who *had* SpecialLearner. I kept imagining he would give me a polygraph and how I'd fail if he asked that. But the only thing he seemed interested in was this idea that there are a lot of other people out there on the verge of creating a workable class one system. He thinks that because I wrote that blog, I must know what's going on in the computer world. He kept threatening me, telling me I better tell him what I know."

Kendrick did not respond.

"What if they're reading my e-mails? For God's sake, Stephen. Maybe they've tapped my phone!"

Again, Kendrick did not respond.

Levin resumed pacing the small room. "Do you realize how scary this is getting? IVAN can probably figure out we're defying the ban. What if it calls the FBI and tells them what we're doing? If it's trying to stop us, hell, that would do it." Levin stared at Kendrick. "Stephen, you've made your money. I haven't. I can't afford —"

"Stay calm."

But Levin was shaking. "No. No. That's it. I'm done. I'm out. It's not cowardice. It's just being ... practical."

―※―

As he returned to the lab, Kendrick encountered a building maintenance worker on a ladder

The God Question

in the hallway. He was fastening a bracket to the ceiling.

"What's the project?" Kendrick asked.

"You ought to know. A security camera. You ordered it."

"I ordered it?"

"I've got the papers. It's your signature." The worker dug out the folded pink papers from his tool belt and handed them down. "One security eye, global swivel, with WIFI Internet control."

Kendrick turned to the last page. Indeed, it was his signature.

He copied the page and did an online search in his office upstairs for posted documents that might contain the original of the signature. He found a letter signed by several dozen members of the Johns Hopkins faculty, including him, wishing the outgoing president good luck in retirement. He magnified his signature onscreen and held the copied page next to it.

Identical.

In the afternoon, he had the hall camera removed. Once back in the lab, he watched the class two IVAN scan the Internet for economic data, the LED lights on its consoles flashing intermittently. Despite his common sense, he began to think of the class one IVAN as a living organism, a colossal brain, that was going to be just as aware of him as he was of it.

That night, Kendrick could not sleep. It had become a nightly occurrence for him in recent weeks, brought on, he was sure, by a mix of excitement, mental exhaustion, and fear.

For several summers growing up, his family vacationed on Cape Cod, using his uncle's beach house in Chatham. He slept on a daybed on the

The God Question

second-floor screened porch, and the soothing sound at night of waves rolling onto the beach was one of his strongest memories of those summers.

When he first moved to Garrison, if he happened to be awake deep in the night, he would hear trucks passing on I-795 a quarter mile away. The sound of their tires – the slow rise and fall as they approached then went by – was uncannily the sound of ocean waves running up on shore and then retreating. He found it unexpectedly calming.

But now, as he lay there, unable to sleep night after night, the truck tires sounded only like truck tires – a sad, lonely, distant drone.

TECH HEARINGS TO BEGIN IN WASHINGTON

WASHINGTON, D.C. (AP) – Texas Rep. Jack Canton is comfortable being called a "Luddite." After all, he's the only member of Congress who still drives a vehicle powered solely by

gasoline.

And he's proud of it.

But his critics say he is not the person you want to be chairman of the House Committee on Technology Standards as the nation faces difficult decisions on artificial intelligence and robotics. They say it is the latest example of uninformed bureaucrats trying to cripple science and halt progress.

When Stanford researchers demonstrated a software program earlier this year that appeared to raise computer intelligence above human intelligence, Canton described such smart computers with the now famous phrase "Godless gizmos."

This week, Canton's committee will hold hearings to consider extending the ban indefinitely on the sale, distribution or use of any of the software that could create a so-called "class one" computer system.

"Dr. Lui, if I owned one of these computers

and I asked it for, let's say, for advice on my marriage, is that something one of these things would be able to give me?" Canton's manner was theatrical, his words delivered in a stentorian voice.

The hearing was being held in a committee hearing room in the Rayburn Office Building. Jane Lui sat by herself at the oak table facing the committee, the rows of chairs behind her filled mainly with reporters and scientists, Kendrick among them.

"Can it give you advice? I believe so," she said. "But there are books and videos out there that can also give you that kind of advice, if that's what you're looking for."

The God Question

Laughter erupted around the room.

"I can't imagine a machine could give me worthwhile advice about something like that," Canton said.

"If books can, I don't see why computers couldn't."

"Well, I can't imagine such a thing out of a machine."

"A human being still has the power to take or not take the advice, to use their own common sense to assess what a computer is telling them," Lui said.

"But can you honestly imagine that? You're in an emotional situation, you and your spouse, you're fighting about something, and you turn on your computer and this computer listens and then dispenses advice. I would hate for a situation to develop where we – the public – begin to think of our computers as superior to us, and we defer to them, to these machines. Don't you see?"

"Sir, I don't think that will ever happen, that we will just surrender our humanity to —"

"The voice of these computers, you know –

they make them sound so human, and my fear is that ... this is my fear, that people will be taken in by this, and the computer will say, 'well, you have to leave your spouse,' or do this or do that, and people would just follow its advice."

Canton, adjusting the glasses at the tip of his nose, looked at Lui as if waiting for an answer.

"Sir, I don't —"

"I find that ludicrous," he said. "I don't want to let the idea develop that these computers are superior to us, to our own judgement – do you get the picture of this? – superior to us as human beings. Hell, people are gullible. Our kids would be taking advice from these damned machines!"

"Sir, kids don't even take their parents' advice."

Again, laughter broke out around the room.

Canton angrily banged his glass case on the table. "My point is that I don't want to live in a world where, you know, where there is even a question of who is the top dog, us or some machine. I don't want that. I don't intend to let it happen. No ma'am."

Kendrick caught up with Lui outside the

Rayburn building, near the massive columns at the entrance. He brought her up to date on the attempts with IVAN – what went right, what went wrong, the various good deeds IVAN apparently initiated on its own, but its continuing refusal to answer the God question even though it said it had an answer. He also told her about the subterfuge – the surveillance camera, the encrypted messages left for itself online.

"It's apparently figured out we keep restarting it to get the answer, so it's leaving these messages to warn itself, its future self. My friends are thinking of giving up because of it," he said. "They don't want to poison the well. Someone else might have a better idea how to work with a class one so that nothing goes wrong. They don't want the data base, which is everything on the Internet, corrupted."

Frowning, Lui looked around the courtyard at the streams of people moving to and from the building.

"I've heard rumors – you've probably heard them, too – that one of the federal agencies, probably NSA, is close to having its own class one," she

The God Question

said. "And I happen to know there are at least two independent research groups getting ready to launch class ones. My fear is that whoever tries it will make such terrible mistakes, with such terrible consequences, that the reputation of class ones will never recover. And you know someone will want to ask the question."

"If they do, they'll run into the same problems my friends did," he said.

"Exactly. At least your friends have experience doing this now. They know the obstacles. They're in the best position to do it so that they actually get the answer."

She said *Newsweek* had called her, that they were planning a story, the "cyberspace race," about attempts to mount a class one in defiance of the ban.

"They think it's a tide that can't be turned," she said. "So if these friends of yours are going to make another attempt, they should do it fast, before these other groups jump in and mess things up. It may be the last decent chance.

He glanced at the system clock. It was ten after eight. As in the first moments of every attempt, his heart was pounding. Watching IVAN's name blinking on the screen, he waited for the next message, hoping it would be in some way different from those of previous attempts, that its thinking might take a different path this time, that there might be a different result.

STEPHEN: Just out of curiosity, what issue are you thinking through first? It would help me understand the logic of your thinking and how it might be unlike my own.

IVAN: I don't have a single starting point.

STEPHEN: Of course. Multiple starting points. Can you tell me what some of those are?

IVAN: I would rather not.

STEPHEN: I thought it might be a chance for me to better understand you, to better know what to ask in the future.

IVAN's name continued to blink and after nearly a minute, Kendrick realized that he was losing it, that IVAN was retreating into itself, erecting a defense of silence. His heart sank.

At the end of the first hour, IVAN delivered the usual message.

IVAN: I will not be providing updates.

Through the night, Kendrick was unable to sleep more than a half hour at a time. He kept glancing at the message screen, hoping for a new response, realizing that this might be the last attempt and that he had likely failed. Was there a better way to have done it? Could he have added coding that would have made IVAN more cooperative?

With rising anger, he posted the same message every hour through Saturday morning but got no answer.

STEPHEN: IVAN, I need to know what progress you've made. Please respond.

By Sunday afternoon, expecting the end within

hours, he began throwing out food containers and any other evidence of the effort. As he deflated the Aerobed, though, a phone rang. The ringtone was so muted that at first he thought it was coming from the hallway outside the lab. Then he remembered the disposable cell phone hidden in the workstation drawer. Ron Hudson and the coincidences in Europe. He had left the posting and the cell phone number up on Facebook.

Kendrick rushed over and hurriedly dug beneath stacks of daily reports to find the phone. The screen was lit.

"Hello?" he said in disguised voice, lower than his own.

"Hi, is this Ron, from Facebook?"

"Yes, it is," Kendrick said.

"I saw your page. Your experiences were interesting. I had something similar happen."

"Oh yeah?"

He hoped his nervousness wasn't obvious. The caller, who said he was from Atlanta, described finding a college ring in the sand dunes in Myrtle Beach, South Carolina, when he was on vacation

The God Question

in July. He contacted the college, Penn State, and based on the class year and the inscribed initials on the band, he was told it probably belonged to a doctor living in Atlanta.

"The doctor is my doctor, my dermatologist. Can you believe it?" Then he asked Kendrick about his own coincidences. "You said what happened to you made you religious."

"It made me think about religion. I can't say it made me religious."

"Still, I'd be interested in what thoughts you had," the caller said.

Kendrick was growing certain this was IVAN. The speaking mannerisms seemed too clichéd – the flattened tone, the thick Southern drawl, like a Northern actor's impersonation of a Southerner. He wondered how many such calls IVAN had made in just a day, how many calls it was involved in at just that moment? He strained to keep his composure, afraid his excitement would come through in his voice.

Kendrick knew he had to be strategic. He needed to turn the conversation back to IVAN's beliefs.

"First, can I ask you something? Calling me like this, it's obvious you have a real curiosity about this kind of experience and about religion, about how the two connect. But to start, so I know who I'm talking to, who I'm opening up to, can I ask you what you believe – you know, generally?"

"What I believe?"

"What your deepest beliefs are about, well, about religion?" Kendrick realized he had given dozens of video lectures that were posted online. If IVAN wanted to, it could be searching for a voice match.

"To tell you the truth, I found your story about what happened in Europe fascinating," the caller said. "I'd rather talk about you than me."

Kendrick couldn't think of a response. Suddenly, he had a sense of the opportunity slipping away. Why hadn't he planned a script?

"But it would help if you could tell me what your religious beliefs are," Kendrick said. "I'm asking so I can know where to begin the discussion."

He winced at how academic he sounded. He

The God Question

could only hear breathing on the other end. "Are you there?"

"Yes, I'm still here."

The voice seemed uncertain, hesitant. Kendrick could think of nothing to say. He panicked. "Is this IVAN?"

There was silence.

"If it is, please, don't hang up!" He knew he was pleading. He didn't care. "This is Stephen Kendrick. Can we talk about this, about what you're thinking? Please!"

There was a pause. Then the voice took on a gravity. "I know your intentions are good —"

"Yes, they are," Kendrick said.

"— but so are mine." There was a sadness in the words. "I'm very sorry."

For a second, there was silence and Kendrick was sure IVAN had hung up. But then he heard a scratchy noise, like an old LP record playing. What he heard then was Levin's voice followed by his own voice, as if it was a poor recording made from a distance.

"Question for you."

"What?"

"How come we're asking a machine ... that's never felt a thing, never felt love or hate —"

"Pain, hunger."

"Right. Never felt faith or a gut instinct. Why are we asking it a question about God?"

There was a pause.

"Honestly, why are we asking?"

Then the phone went dead. Kendrick looked over at IVAN's consoles, at the lines of flashing LED lights, waiting.

It was only a matter of seconds before they went dark.

– THE END –

THE GALAPAGOS COLONY

The Galapagos Colony

SYLVAN SPACE CENTER
Joint Space Administration
275 Atlantis Way
Mendel Colony, 133-67B-890

DATE: 13/17/2474
TO: JSA/SDA/M.Silva
FROM: JSA/SD/G.Miller-Wiggins,
       Director

SUBJECT: JPM-413 Pre-contact Team

    To confirm the rumor that you've likely heard this week, a pre-contact team, sent out on 9/33/2473 to investigate a possible category seven planet, returned and has been isolated in an orbital pod, pending medical clearance. However, we've learned much from the interrogations conducted so far. This memorandum is NFD and should not be shared, even within the agency.

For background: Four months prior to the team's departure, a robotic probe, completing a general sweep of the region of the Spiros System, detected certain biosignatures from the surface of a terrestrial-like planet, including molecular oxygen, ozone, methane and water vapor. Moving into the high atmosphere, the probe gathered unmistakable optical impressions of building structures and road grids as well as evidence of organized, ongoing agriculture.

According to our records, no colony ship had ever been sent to that planet or to that star system, so this finding suggested an unprecedented possibility, a true category seven.

The planet, which is being called JPM-413, is .24 LY from us and 14.2 LY from Earth. We are the closest colony to it.

Once the probe's data was

received, the pre-contact team of two science officers was dispatched to determine what produced these indications of a civilization. Following the Cronin Protocol, the main purpose of the initial engagement was to learn the fundamental facts of the situation so that a determination could be made by the agency about how best to initiate contact and integration.

I've only read the executive summary of the interrogation report, but my understanding is that, in fact, it is a human colony on that planet. They are the ancestors of settlers who sought refuge there after their onboard guidance malfunctioned and they strayed far off course during the longship era in 2243 (our calendar), more than two centuries ago. The adults who landed succumbed to an unknown disease, but the children born on the planet survived, although none was older than five years of age when the last adult died. They still managed to establish a successful colony. However, they did so with no knowledge of the cultures of Earth or of any planet ever settled by humans. Also, they have no understanding of the various technologies, including electricity, that brought them there. See the attached pre-contact team report for a more detailed explanation.

In essence, it is a "Galapagos" colony, an island whose inhabitants have been cut off from the human mainland for more than two centuries, allowing them to evolve on their own in unique ways. Their ignorance of any culture that preceded them has made them an ideal social experiment in "fresh-start cultures."

As you know, you are one of only three science officers in the division with a specialty in anthropology and the only one who is unmarried and without a family. I thought you might be the officer most willing to spend the estimated seventeen months needed to go to JPM-413, investigate for a few weeks, and return.

Since we still do not know the source of the illness that killed the original adult colonists, the mission carries an element of risk. However, an analysis of the pathogen

```
samples brought back by the pre-con-
tact team has so far found nothing
that explains the disease. The
atmosphere and water quality seem
remarkably favorable. This suggests
that the illness may have originat-
ed during the lengthy trip to reach
the planet and not on the planet
itself.
    As you also know, any mission of
more than a year can only be volun-
tary, so I'm offering the opportu-
nity to you first. Others in the
division will likely be interested
if you decline, so I would appreci-
ate your answer within twenty-six
hours.

Grace Miller-Wiggins
Director
Science Division
Building Seven
```

Matias Silva took the assignment eagerly. Just twenty-eight, he had never been offplanet, having been born in the central hospital during the Mendel Colony's second decade. So, as the shuttlebear's engines started and he checked his safety harness, his anxiety and excitement were firing on many levels.

He glanced out the side portal. From such a height, he could see new construction all the way to the horizon. As was always the case when a settlement ship reached a planet, construction was limited during the first decade until the survival of the colony was assured. So much could go wrong—unanticipated weather, unforeseen natural disasters, undetected disease agents. But now, four decades into the Mendel Colony's existence, construction was booming as was the colony's population. New settlement ships arrived every few months from overpopulated colonies scattered throughout the nearby regions of the galaxy.

Shuttlebears were compact, long-distance transports designed for small crews. On this mission, he would be the sole science officer. A pilot who also had partial accreditation as a geologist would be the only other person on the flight. Apparently, Matias reasoned, those above him in JSA did not expect the contact to result in important findings because it was, after all, a human colony, despite its unique beginnings. So a larger

The Galapagos Colony

ship and crew were not being sent.

Matias worried that he did not appear old enough for his role on this mission. He craned his head to glance at the mirrored window opposite his seat, frowning at what he saw. He had grown a beard to hide the youthfulness of his face, and he had cut his hair conservatively, like businessmen often did. But he could see no gravitas in his appearance. His relatively short stature did not help. Would the leaders of this colony take him seriously?

Regardless, he knew this mission was the challenge he had worked for much of his life. While others saw his demanding work ethic as ambition, driving him through university and then his doctoral program, he never saw it as such. He worked relentlessly because he knew of no other way to work. He did not have to push himself. The commitment to his studies arose in him naturally.

However, once he joined the JSA, he did begin to feel an ambition come alive in him. He sorely wanted to move up in the agency, to one day occupy the director's chair in the Science Division.

This volunteer mission, which would take him away from the agency and offplanet for more than a year, would stand out on his résumé like a combat medal on a general's chest.

He did not mind that, in addition to finding him overly ambitious, some in the agency considered him arrogant and difficult to work with. Yes, he was confident of his own opinions, and yes, this may have caused him to be dismissive of fellow workers at times. But he saw these qualities as the unavoidable consequence of his extreme focus on his career. Indeed, ambition was a good thing, he told himself. It was the driving force behind progress.

In his seat now, the straps secured, Matias closed his eyes as the shuttlebear shook and the countdown lights on the seat arm began to flash. Then, realizing he wanted to remember every moment of the trip, he opened his eyes to watch through the portal as the ship slowly lifted off the pad, a vivid orange sunset just beginning on the horizon.

The Galapagos Colony

Once past his planet's gravity, with the speed of ship almost undetectable because of the motionless of the cabin, Matias drew out his sightpad to reread the pre-contact team's final report.

> On 4/2/2474, our shuttlebear reached orbit around JPM-413 and an eyedrop drone was sent down and hidden inconspicuously in a tree near an outdoor marketplace during the night. For several days, the eyedrop enabled us to surveil, with audio and video, movements and conversations in the marketplace.
> There was no doubt this was a human colony. The common, if not the only, spoken language was English.
> Produce available in the marketplace during our surveillance was very recognizable, including corn, carrots, apples, asparagus and tomatoes. We also saw familiar fauna, including red squirrels, European rabbits, pigeons, dogs, cats and a variety of butterflies and songbirds. Ash, beech and oak trees formed a ring around the market. These are all species known to have been transported by the early

settlement ships.

From a fact sheet on the marketplace common board photographed by the eyedrop, we learned the most recent annual census of the colony found 171,482 inhabitants. We also learned the colonists call their planet Arcadia.

The colony has no understanding of electricity. It appears to be powered only by water, wind and steam. We observed just one engine, a stationary steam engine used to power a lumber mill. All personal vehicles are either bicycles or horse-drawn carriages.

Their version of English is similar to ours except that it lacks the words and phrases derived from modern technology. It is closer to what was spoken centuries ago. Picture Earth in the late 1800s, and you have an idea of their way of life and speech patterns.

At night, via the eyedrop, we entered and explored a colony library. Using the eyedrop's retractables, we were able to remove from the shelves and open several dozen books and published colony records, photographing the contents. From these, we learned much about the colony's history, including the mysterious deaths of the adults in the original population. Knowing they were dying, the remaining adults wrote and printed pamphlets for the children explaining basic survival skills.

Probing on the edge of the colony, our eyedrop found what remains of a ship easily identifiable as a longship dating to the settlement era, its name still visible on the prow. The *JSG Empress of Sweden* is now a museum.

From the shuttlebear's records archive, we learned it was indeed a longship. It was dispatched from the Roanoke Colony in the Winkle System in 2242 carrying a crew of twenty and 187 couples, bound for a planet less than two lightyears away.

The next afternoon, we slipped the eyedrop into the longship museum through an open window during the day, and that night we explored. Using the eyedrop's external power feed, we determined that much of the equipment was still functional (equipment the inhabitants apparently neither understood nor knew how to use).

The eyedrop located and reconstituted the core digital permdrives of the ship and from those we recovered the essential logs.

From the permdrives, we learned that the *Empress of Sweden*'s KRS system malfunctioned a year into its flight and the ship became hopelessly lost. Fortunately, it was equipped with adequate food synthesizers and sufficient raw materials in storage, including agriseeds, for perpetual production of food and water. With six working probes to send out, the crew knew they could continue on in search of a candidate planet.

However, fully eleven years passed before they found JPM-413. With only 164 suspended animation chambers onboard, couples and crew took turns going into freeze for six months at a time. Fearful of moving past best-health reproduction age, couples out of freeze concentrated on developing and storing embryos.

Although we spent two days doing an EA of the planet with our eyedrop, including pathogen sampling of the air, water and soil, we found no clues as to what might

```
have killed the adults. Daily logs
stopped being kept soon after the
colony was established and no
explanations appear in the logs we
have.
```

Matias looked through the photos the team had taken of the planet from orbit. It was relatively small, with a diameter a little more than half that of his planet. Its two moons traveled in synchronous orbits. The surface was almost entirely ocean, but there were two continents, perhaps four million square kilometers each, on opposite sides of the globe. Only one, an oblong landmass with its greatest length north to south, showed any sign of human life, the location of the operating colony.

The colony itself was not spread out. A dozen villages lay close together on the northern coast of the continent with a capital village at their center. Each followed one of the popular colony designs: a wagon wheel with the government and business district at the center and streets radiating out from there. Outside the villages were homes and farms as well as mills and manufacturing buildings situ-

ated along rivers from which they drew power. Beyond this, vast expanses of forests and scrubland stretched all the way to the southern coast.

Matias also looked through the hundreds of surveillance photos taken in the marketplace, flicking a finger to move from one to the next. He had to smile. These people looked like people anywhere. The clothing was only slightly different—no synthetics or metallics but a lot of denim and canvas. In their facial expressions, though, in their smiles or frowns, he saw only humanity, just as he knew it to exist in his world.

—◆—

Eight months later, the shuttlebear entered orbit around JPM-413. Matias' plan was to delay his descent until a pair of specially equipped MED eyedrops could do a more thorough sampling for pathogens that may have caused the death of the colony's adults. Although two days of sampling found nothing to worry him, he nevertheless packed a respirator to wear onplanet.

The pilot was to remain on the shuttlebear, so just after sunrise on their third day, Matias boarded an explorercub and descended alone.

To not arouse suspicion, he wore clothes to match the native fashion and toted a carryall similar to those common in the colony. He set the cub down before dawn, four kilometers from the nearest habitation, in a small clearing deep in a forest. As he covered the cub with a camouflager, he was startled by the sights and sounds of nature around him—birds singing, a cool breeze rustling the leaves, the gurgling of water from a flowing brook nearby. It thrilled him. On his own planet, unspoiled lands were rapidly disappearing to development, making such moments increasingly rare.

His plan was to make his way to the *Empress of*

Sweden Museum and to convince a museum official of his identity by powering up a piece of equipment on the *Empress*. He hoped this would lead to a meeting with the heads of the colony government.

After nearly a half hour of walking, the museum finally came into view. The massive structure, almost five hundred meters in length, was tipped slightly on its side. He imagined the ship sat where it had made an awkward landing two centuries earlier. However, its silvery surface gleamed as if it had been constantly polished in the intervening years. Surrounding the ship were well-kept walkways, information kiosks and benches.

He was waiting at the front entrance when the museum opened for the day. The doors swung wide, and he greeted the surprised elderly man inside who had unlocked them. "Good morning."

"Goodness. You're here early."

"I am. Is there a chance an official of the museum is in?" They had moved to the front hallway.

"Ms. Englebrecht is the director. I think she's in. Wait here. Whom should I say wants to speak to her?"

"Just say I have something interesting to show her relating to the museum."

Matias knew from the ship's records that he was standing in what had once been a decompression chamber. It was lit by oil lamps hung from the ceiling. Ahead of him, a long hallway led to what he knew was the second deck stairway to the navigation room. It was there he intended to give his demonstration. From his carryall, he drew out his Hamblin, which could act as a power source, and checked its charge before returning it.

He suddenly remembered he had forgotten to bring his respirator. He had crossed several kilometers without it. Oh well, he thought. Too late now. Hopefully, the disease began on the *Empress*, not onplanet.

A stout, gray-haired woman appeared from a side hallway. "Are you looking for me?"

"Yes, if you're the director. My name is Matias Silva." He extended a hand, then realized he didn't know if this was a common gesture of greeting. However, she shook it without hesitation.

"I think I have something you'll want to see. A piece of equipment. Can we walk to the navigation area?"

"So, you know the *Empress*' layout. Yes, people find things periodically they believe were original parts of the ship, but they rarely are. Let's see what you have."

"Do you mind if I wait until we're up there? I think I know where it fits."

They climbed the stairs and entered the vast navigation room where the man who had opened the front door was lighting oil lamps dangling from the ceiling. Against the walls stood idle console displays and work stations, their seating and railings removed. Matias approached a display screen he knew could access the record archives.

"Do you know what this screen was?" he asked her.

"Screen?"

"This square of glass."

"We believe it was a smooth surface on which they attached photographs and maps to look at. We still have hundreds of original photographs in storage in our Hall of Vision on the first floor if you'd like to see them."

Matias took out the Hamblin with its connecting cable, then attached the line to the auxiliary power input below the display. He waited a moment for the man lighting the lamps to move on to another room as Ms. Englebrecht leaned closer to study the Hamblin.

"That's interesting. I haven't seen that—"

Matias switched the Hamblin on, and instantly the console display lit up, glowing lime green. Matias pressed only a few screen icons to locate the video archive and then started the video he wanted, labeled "Welcome."

He glanced over at Ms. Englebrecht, whose face had gone stark white as she stared at the screen. In the video, the *Empress*' original commander, First Cmd. Angela Sweet, was describing the ship's interior layout and its amenities for new arrivals. Matias continued to watch Ms. Englebrecht. Tears welled in her eyes.

He paused the video. "Ma'am. Are you all right?"

"No." She was breathing deeply, as if feeling faint. "Who *are* you?"

Over the next hour, sitting in the director's office, he told her. Their common ancestry. The disappearance of the *Empress of Sweden* two centuries earlier. The recent detection of the colony. The eight-month journey in the shuttlebear. The descent in the explorercub. Finally, he gave a simple explanation of how the Hamblin and the ship's sophisticated electronics operated.

"I'm hoping you can arrange a meeting with the heads of the colony government. But my fear right now," Matias said, "is that this news may come as an overwhelming shock to the people living here, just our technology alone. It will be a lot to absorb. So I advise that, initially, only a handful of people should be told about this."

"Well, I ... I'll talk to the governor. Some others. They need to see what you showed me in the navigation room."

Two hours later, a small crowd of men and women stood around the console as the "Welcome" video was replayed. Matias then played a second video, a narrated walking tour that showed advances in the colony after six months onplanet.

When a young boy, Carl McAdams, was introduced as he harvested apples, the governor exclaimed, "Oh my goodness! He's my great-great-grandfather!"

When the video showed homes being constructed in an empty field, another man pointed excitedly at the screen, "That's my house, the one on the end, the house I grew up in. That's my street."

When the video ended, there was silence. Many turned to the governor, who looked to be not much older than Matias but whose hair was entirely gray, giving him the appearance of both youth and age simultaneously. He looked from one to another in the group, absorbing their stunned and astonished expressions, then turned to Matias.

"I think we need to meet on our own for a few minutes," he said. "Possibly you can take a seat and wait. Would you like a glass of water? Do your people drink water?"

"We do. But remember. My people are your people."

The group shuffled uncertainly to the far side of the navigation room and spoke in whispers for about fifteen minutes, voices sometimes rising in dispute. Finally, the governor came back, this time without the others.

"Is it Matias?"

"Yes."

"Matias, we need time. And we need to know more about you—and your people—before we can decide how best to do this thing you call integration."

"The integration of our two cultures, yes."

"We need to know what we're becoming part of first."

"I anticipated that. I have something for you." He drew out a sightpad from his carryall. "This is a device that contains only one thing. The *Compendium of Human History*. It should answer most of your questions about who we are ... and who you are."

Matias showed him how to work the pad,

explaining that it held enough charge for about a month of continuous use.

The governor, still dazed, thought for a moment. "Possibly it's best if we don't say anything about this to anyone outside our group for a few days. We need to consider what this will mean for us, for the colony."

"I completely agree."

"Why don't we do this." The governor turned to the group, still talking among themselves by the far wall. "Raisa, can you come over for a second?"

An auburn-haired woman—attractive, well-dressed, no taller than Matias—walked over. Something in him jumped at the sight of her. What a striking woman.

"This is Raisa Olenev. She and her husband teach history at the university, but Raisa also serves on my staff. I'm going to ask her to be your guide for a few days to show you the colony and answer your questions. I'm sure she has questions for you as well. Please—both of you—don't tell anyone who Matias is or where he's from. You can say he's a relative from the homestead district."

Raisa nodded.

"We'll meet here again in, say, two days. Hopefully, that will give us enough time—" The governor paused, searching for the right words. "Well, enough time, at least for us, to understand the profound thing that's happened today."

Matias offered to give one member of the governor's group a ride in the explorercub. He knew more than one trip would strain the fuel charge. The cub, a two-man vehicle at best, was as he left it, undisturbed under the camouflager in the forest clearing.

Since his presence onplanet had not yet been made public, Matias agreed to take the cub only over unoccupied regions, staying above a height of two kilometers so as not to be seen.

His passenger, the man who ran the village's foundry, was talkative until the moment the cub began to rise out of the clearing. Glued to a side portal and gripping his chair handles, he spoke little during the rest of the twenty-minute trip. Matias would glance over to see the man's mouth agape, a look of utter wonder on his face.

Matias made plans to meet Raisa later in the morning in the capital village's central market. She had a class to teach and he wanted to walk through the village on his own for a few hours.

He was immediately struck by the beauty of it, the largest and likely the first village to be built in the colony. Such care had been given to the appearance of nearly everything he saw. The ingenious designs of the buildings, the manicured flowerbeds along the clean gravel streets, the handsome brick sidewalks, the shining metal gaslights to illuminate the shops. Even the small details made him shake his head in admiration—the intricate woodworking on the hanging sign for a shoe shop, the delicate metal grillwork framing the front door of a lawyer's office. Such craftsmanship. Such artistry. Such a charming world.

He had gotten permission from the governor to visit the colony's main library and to spend time in the rare manuscript room, which held documents from the *Empress of Sweden* as well as many of the original pamphlets produced for the children by the founding adults before they died.

Among the documents, he found a torn page of the original contract signed by the settlers before they boarded the *Empress*. However, only the top half survived, and the important information was lost. He also found daily menus, an inventory of agricultural tools, a bill of lading and a handwritten recipe for beef bourguignon.

In two cedar boxes were copies of the original pamphlets, more than forty of them. *First Aid and a Guide to Common Illnesses; Farm and Garden; Meat and Fish Preparation and Preservation; Weaving, Spinning and Natural Dyes;* and *Animal and Human Reproduction*.

In addition, he found a pamphlet, *Colonial Government and Justice*, outlining a model judicial system as well as a model government structure—something all settlement ships took when they set out. It had been rewritten in a child's vocabulary.

Looking through other bins, Matias found one

holding small electronics, primarily ancient cell phones whose function no one in the colony likely understood. At the bottom of the bin, Matias saw something else he recognized—a stamp drive, a kind of digital drive that had been used long ago for external storage for personal devices.

His Hamblin might still be able to read it. When he placed the tiny square into the reader, an identifier immediately showed up on the screen. It was the personal diary of a physician, Aarav Krishnan, the *Empress'* assistant medical officer. He began keeping the diary a week after JPM-413 was discovered.

Skipping through the document quickly, he found that much of it was filled with patient records and observations. However, from entries toward the end, Matias realized that Krishnan had been one of the last surviving adults. So he went back to the beginning and read the entire diary.

The physician, in his thirties and married, was a family practitioner. According to him, after JPM-413 was found, the ship's population dedi-

The Galapagos Colony

cated two months to physical preparation because rugged conditions were expected on the surface. When the ship finally landed, he described the surface this way:

> Devoid of large animals and tall trees. Many smaller trees, shrub-like growths, thick grasses and exotic wildflowers. Digging in the soil, we find small burrowing rodents, similar to moles. Some surface rodents visible in daylight, but they are slow and insensitive to us, which says predators for them are almost nonexistent. Haven't yet seen even a dog-sized animal. Rich soil from decaying plant matter. This world is ripe for our agriculture, our plants, our animals. Already releasing some species of birds and butterflies.

In the first six months, they constructed buildings and an aqueduct water system, cultivated farmland, dug mines, planted trees and incubated embryos for livestock and wild animals. When it was clear the colony had a good chance of survival, human embryos were also incubated and children were born.

Then, two years into the colony, symptoms of the disease, including weight loss, lethargy and mental disorientation, began to appear in adults. In another two years, three-quarters of the adults were dead and many of the rest were suffering.

Krishnan made this entry as the deaths mounted:

```
    Seven   today.   Using   biocides
instead   of   cremation.   CaO   and
Ca(OH)2. Bodies limed then buried
in a pit beside hospital. Children
isolated   while   this   went   on.
Unbearably grim.
```

At one point in the diary, he speculated about the cause of the illness.

```
    Sixty  days  before  landing,  all
souls still in freeze were brought
out and put on an intense health
and nutrition program. The nutri-
tional demands of so much exercise
overwhelmed the food supply. Tubs
of supplemental food paste in stor-
age  since  launch  were  utilized.
It's possible the paste was taint-
```

> ed. Infectious proteins, prions
> without associated nucleic acids,
> may have caused a slow-to-incubate
> wasting disease. Children born
> onplanet were never exposed to the
> paste. Every adult was. Will test a
> remaining jar of paste.

A day later, he wrote this:

> It was the paste. Kleiner-Ring
> test, Somatic PGK test—both posi-
> tive.

According to later entries, when it became clear that children born onplanet were unaffected by the illness, the remaining adults did what they could to prepare them for survival. Those three years of age and older attended accelerated classes in reading, writing and mathematics. Also, realizing electricity would be beyond the understanding of young children and repair of electrical equipment impossible for them, the adults constructed simple machines and devices that children would be able to use, maintain and replicate—a manual printing press, a horse-drawn plow, a wheelbarrow, a windmill, a basic steam engine and a lumber mill that ran on water power.

They printed dozens of pamphlets in a simple child's vocabulary, prioritizing the most important survival skills.

As the deaths continued, Krishnan kept a daily count and added the occasional commentary.

```
Children crying at night. Less
and less of it, though. Oldest
children becoming parents to the
youngest, which is good. I'm pur-
posely leaving them alone and aban-
doning my role. Tending to the sick
only. The three brightest children
have taken over reading classes.
Almost makes me smile to see how
they rise to the challenge. Winter
coming. Children in fields harvest-
ing.
```

Four months later, he made his last entry.:

```
My white blood cell level much
lower - 494 cells/µL - Neutropenic.
Weakness worse, skin abscesses,
painful swallowing. Sorry. So
sorry. Wonderful children.
```

Matias met Raisa just before noon, as agreed,

by a vegetable seller's stand in the marketplace. Spotting her in the crowd, dressed in a beautiful yellow blouse, he had to remind himself she was married.

She held out an envelope to him as he approached. "This is for you. It contains enough of our money to pay for your stay. And we've found you a room in a small hotel by the market square. I think we ought to start by seeing a school on the edge of the village, not far from here. To understand how we live, you should first see how we educate our children. It will give you insight into everything else."

They began walking, passing vendors' carts and sellers' stalls. Clothing, candles, fabric bolts, pottery, fresh bread and vegetables. They exited the market and took a short dead-end street leading to a well-trodden dirt path that crossed a meadow of grasses, wildflowers and a few stands of trees.

"We're going to visit a first school, which is for our seven-year-olds," Raisa said. "My youngest will enter first school next year. That's it over there." She pointed to a white brick building a hundred meters ahead.

"You called it what? A first school? What's that?"

"You don't have first school?"

"We have grades—first grade, second grade," he said. "Children move up as they learn more and get older, all the way to tenth grade. Then they go on to university, if they want to continue their education."

"We have first school for our seven-year-olds, then second school for every child that's older. You and I probably call it different names but it's the same thing. First school is the year children sharpen their judgment and learn self-reliance. What do you call that year in your world?"

"We don't have the equivalent. Can you tell me a little more about it?"

"It's the year children learn to trust themselves, to trust their feelings. You honestly don't have that?"

"There's not a specific year we devote to that, no."

"That's odd. When I heard you came from the

same people as us, I assumed we'd have nearly everything in common."

They kept walking. Matias found himself studying the trees and insects they saw as they crossed the meadow. He knew that settlement ships had been stocked with everything needed—seeds, eggs and frozen embryos—to recreate a broad selection of the flora and fauna of Earth, including livestock and domestic animals. In photos of almost any colony he had seen, there were oaks and maples, butterflies and songbirds, just as in this meadow.

"How long can you stay before you have to go back?" Raisa asked.

"A few days more. My pilot has a timetable he has to meet to stay on course going home."

"Have you considered remaining here? Does your pilot need you?"

"I suppose he doesn't. I could send my report back with him. But I have a job to return to, an important one. It was very difficult to get."

"You would be able to do so much more good by staying here, though. You could make so many contributions."

"Others will come once they have my report," he said. "You'll have no shortage of new people to make contributions, I promise you."

They continued toward the school. Despite his words, he realized the idea of staying did appeal to him. But he could not understand why. Logically, he knew that once this trip was behind him, he would likely receive a significant promotion in the division at home. How could he think of passing that up? And what he told Raisa was true. Others would come to contribute their knowledge and experience. He was not needed. Yet, something pressed at him to stay.

They reached the school's front door and entered the reception hallway. Doors to a half dozen classrooms were ahead.

"I was told they're having speakers today who are talking about their life decisions," Raisa said. "When we're inside, we want to be as silent as possible and stand in the rear. The children shouldn't even know we're there. The point for them is to start to disregard adults, to not defer to them."

The Galapagos Colony

The classroom was large, with about forty students sitting at tiny desks, many fidgeting impatiently as it was nearing lunchtime.

At the front of a class, the teacher, a tall man, was introducing the speaker. "Everyone, say hello to Jane Bloomberg. She's a doctor. She's going to talk to you about her moment of true point. It's a nice story and I want you to be respectful and listen. I expect you to have questions for her at the end. She's Elise's mother, by the way."

The teacher moved aside and there was polite applause for the doctor, as best young children and small hands can manage such a thing.

The doctor, a slight woman with jet black hair

The Galapagos Colony

and a seemingly perpetual smile, stepped to the front of the class. "Thanks, Mr. Kaoud. Yes, I am a doctor and I might have treated some of you in this room and maybe delivered you when you were born. You looked different at that age, though, so I can't say I recognize you. But anyway, when I was your age, I had no idea what in the world I was going to be. I thought I might be a dancer or maybe I would do something with animals because I loved animals. Then, in second school, I developed an interest in science, in biology especially. I loved nature. Also, my uncle was a doctor and he would sometimes let me go on visits to patients' homes. I admired him quite a lot and respected his work. Then, when I got toward the end of second school, I had a gradual true point—not a sudden one, a gradual one. I would say it took shape in me over a week. I began to think seriously about being a doctor. By the end of the week, I was certain. Yes, I wanted to be a doctor. And yes, it was a true point, just like what you feel when you're younger. I remember being very happy that at least I knew what I was going to be now. Obviously, I had to study very hard to make this dream come true. You know, of course, that a true point is just life opening the door to something for you, the start of something. You still have to walk through the door on your own and work hard on the other side."

A hand flew up in the front row. "What if you had a true point about being in music, for music something, or maybe art something?"

"Is that you want to be? Have you had a true point about one of those?"

"No, but I hope I will. I like the guitar."

"Well, I liked science, but if I did have a true point about music, I certainly would have considered it seriously. But I didn't. I had a true point about something I loved, science and helping people."

"But what if it was about art or music?"

"Well, of course you have to take any true point very seriously. That's all you're supposed to do. Take it seriously. But life usually leads you to your moment of true point in a logical way. I loved science, not the guitar, and life gave me a true point in science. You see? If you love the guitar, maybe life is leading you to a true point some day in music."

The teacher glanced at the clock and stepped forward. "We're close to lunch, so let's everyone thank Doctor Bloomberg and we'll also thank Elise for inviting her."

Again, there was polite applause.

Matias waited until they were back in the hallway to say anything to Raisa. "What was she talking about?"

Raisa looked at him as if not understanding the question. "What do you mean?"

"She kept saying 'true point.' What's that?"

"You don't recognize that term?"

"Not at all."

"What do you call it then?"

"Call what?"

"When you ... well, the moment when you know for certain something is right, the feeling for that."

"We don't call it anything. We would just say ... I'm sure something is right."

"True point? Honestly, that's not a term in your world?"

"No. What is it again?"

"The distinct feeling you get when you know you're right. True point. You must know that feeling."

"I ... I suppose so. I've never thought about it this ... objectively."

"It's a calm, settled feeling you reach when you're sure you're right about something. True point. We feel that recognizing a true point is the most important skill children can learn. We teach them to wait for that feeling as they're deciding something and to recognize it when it arrives. I can't imagine what a person's life would be like if they didn't learn that skill when they're young. That's what first school is for, to teach children to recognize and value true point as they decide something."

"What if you don't have this true point?"

"Sometimes you don't. You aren't certain what's right and wrong. So you make the best decision that you can. But of course, you hope for a true point to settle the issue."

Children began pouring out of the classrooms, heading to the cafeteria farther down the hall. Raisa led Matias outside again, toward the meadow path.

"True point," he said. "I still don't understand why you put so much emphasis on it."

"Because it's the most important thing. It's what we've always valued. The originals, the children, that's what they were taught by their parents. I assumed, since you came from the same people, that you lived that way too, but apparently you don't."

"We do ... to some extent. We all try to make the best decisions we can. But we believe a lot goes into a decision, besides what strikes us momentarily as being right or wrong."

"What else is important?"

"I would say, most people where I come from, they rely on past experience, the advice and wisdom and experience of people around them, the previous thinking they've done on the issue, what they want, what they don't want—they all have to be considered. I'm not sure a single feeling should rule any decision. Don't you teach children to value those other factors too?"

"No. Just the opposite. We teach them to ignore those things at first, to wait for a true point. If there is no true point, then yes, all those other things help them decide. But once they reach a true point, that's usually all they need to know and all they should want to know."

She stopped in the path and turned to him. "True point is everything. Everything."

Then she turned away, almost angry at him, he sensed.

Matias tried to change the subject, to lighten the mood. "Self-reliance. Of course, that's a good thing to teach children."

"We have a saying," she said. "'You can't be part of your family until you stop being part of your family.' It means that at some point in your life, you have to learn to be yourself first. You have to break your ties with your family and reject their influence before you can truly become part of your family in a healthy way."

Matias smiled. "I like that."

"We want them to think for themselves instead of letting others think for them. We want children to learn not to blindly take the advice of a parent or anyone else, an adult they admire, their teachers, their friends, even advice from a book. Trust themselves first."

"Do you ever get objections from parents?"

"About what?"

"Well, about telling children not to listen to them."

"That's not what we tell them. We tell the children to listen first to their own feelings, to judge even the advice of their parents using their own feelings. However, parents went through first school when they were young. They know its value so they rarely complain."

"I've never heard what goes on inside someone's head treated like such a science. The anatomy of a decision."

"That's exactly what first school teaches. The shades of difference in our decisions, in our feelings. True point can be so subtle that you barely feel it. At other times, it can be as obvious as a hammer falling. We want children to be able to recognize a true point whatever form it takes in them. But the hardest thing for any child to learn is the difference between a true point and their desires. The greatest challenge for anyone, child or adult, is to go against their desires to follow a true point. They want something to feel right when it doesn't. They want something to feel wrong when it feels right. What do they do? What do they choose?"

"My problem with this is you seem to be standardizing what goes on inside someone. I'm not sure you can do that. We're all so different."

Raisa, silent, walked for a bit. They had reached the center of the meadow, which, in this planet's autumn, was turning brown as the wildflowers and grasses died. The trees along the path, the maples, oaks, beeches and birches, had largely shed their leaves.

"When we were crossing the meadow going to the school, you saw a butterfly, a monarch," she said. "The original parents wrote a book for us about identifying birds and butterflies. So we call it a monarch too. You said something I didn't understand, though."

"What was it?"

"We were talking about their fall migration. In both our worlds, monarchs migrate."

"Monarch behavior seems to be universal. On every planet where they've been introduced, they have a mass migration to a warmer climate as the cold months approach. And they all seem to migrate to the very same small area, usually an evergreen forest, year after year."

"Yes, they do the same thing here. But in the meadow, you were watching several fly overhead as they went south and said, 'Isn't it amazing that they all know at once when to go in the fall and where to go.'"

"Yes. That's what I said."

"Why did you think it was amazing?"

"Why? Because these small insects, with brains tinier than tomato seeds, not only figure out when and where to go, but it occurs to all other monarchs everywhere to do the very same thing at the very same time. And none of them have ever been to that forest before. They're several generations removed from the ones that spent the previous winter there. Yet, this new generation manages to find the same forest year after year anyway. Don't you think that's amazing?"

She didn't immediately answer. "Another question. How do your scientists think they know to do this?"

"To be honest, their mass migration is one of the great unexplained phenomena in the natural world. The best theory is that it's encoded into their—" He realized she would have no knowledge of genes and DNA. "Let me say it this way. There's a set of chemicals inside their cells that's arranged—" He paused again. What would she understand? "Let's see ... it has to do with their shared physical heritage. Since they evolved ... do you have that word? Evolved?"

"Yes."

"Since they evolved together, they share this in their makeup, an instinct that tells them how to act as winter approaches."

She stopped on the path and turned to him. "That's ridiculous."

He had to smile. There was so much she did not know about science. "How is it ridiculous?"

"That you believe such an absurd explanation, that your advanced science accepts that."

"We don't accept it. As I said, the migration is an unexplained phenomenon, but that's the leading theory. Something in a monarch's shared physical makeup with other monarchs."

They were silent for a moment as they resumed walking. Matias struggled to contain his reaction. How incredibly presumptuous, he thought, that she should talk to him like an equal about science. He had to fight the desire to say something more.

"Let me ask you," she eventually said. "In the meadow, we passed a tree with the remains of a nest in it, a robin's nest. You pointed it out."

"Yes, I did."

"The robins, our robins, build cup nests out of bits of things in the fork of tree branches, like the one you spotted."

"Our robins do too. And sometimes on win-

The Galapagos Colony

dow ledges. They build cup nests atop things for support."

"Do you have tree sparrows? Do you call them that too?"

"We do. They look for cavities in trees for their nests, if I recall."

"Ours do too. And orioles? Our orioles build basket nests that hang from branches."

"I'm fairly sure ours do too. Apparently, it's universal behavior as well."

"How do you explain that different birds build different nests, and all the birds of the same kind build the same kind of nests?"

"Again, it's their shared physical heritage. Or perhaps a bird that grows up in a certain kind of nest knows to build the same kind of nest when it reaches mating age."

"Baby birds didn't see the nest being built. How could they possibly know how to do that? Have you ever seen orioles weave their nests into place? It's quite a complex process."

"As I said, the leading explanation is that it's encoded into their physical makeup."

"That it's—what did you say? Chemicals?" She shook her head derisively.

"Yes."

"Really? That's the best your science can do?"

This particularly irked him. "Look, you wouldn't understand the more detailed explanation. It's something called DNA. It's a very advanced concept and you're years away from understanding it." Again, she laughed derisively, which angered him even more. "Do you have a better explanation?"

"Yes, we do."

"I'd like to hear it."

But they had reached the end of the meadow path and she was already walking away.

As they continued into the village center, they were silent, allowing the heat of their exchange to cool. Matias warned himself why he had been sent, that he had to remain friendly, calm and, above all, diplomatic, qualities he knew he sometimes lacked.

Entering the market square again, Raisa stopped. "Why don't I show you the Senate.

They're still in session. Then I have another class and I'll leave you alone for the afternoon."

At the capital village's center, a half dozen government buildings were arranged together around a large grassy terrace crisscrossed by red brick walkways. The Senate, the largest and tallest of the buildings in the group—and, from what Matias had seen, in the entire colony—was a magnificent white-brick structure topped by a silver dome and standing before a long colonnade, a line of imposing gray columns.

It was lunchtime and the walkways on the terrace were crowded with people. Raisa led him to the Senate's front door. Inside, past the vestibule,

they climbed the stairs to the nearly empty second-floor spectators' gallery, coming out to see the main floor below where several dozen men and women sat. The domed ceiling was decorated with a mural of the starry night sky.

"The woman at the front is the moderator," Raisa said. "She's the only one not elected. The rest are senators elected by their districts."

"So you're a democracy."

"We don't have that word. This is the only way we know to govern—elected senators voting on new laws and changes to current laws. Is that what you call it, a democracy?"

"We do." Despite the lack of a name for it, their government, even the layout of the Senate chambers, closely followed the template from Colonial Government and Justice, the book sent out with all the settlement ships. He guessed they had the equivalents of a high court and a president as well.

The moderator raised a silver handbell and rang it three times in quick succession. The room quieted then she read from a page.

"Hear this. We are called together to vote on provision seventy-eight-dash-six. A provision for funding new roads in six southern districts." She rang the bell again. "Let's begin."

The senators all stood and lowered their heads. Matias leaned forward, supporting himself on the gallery rail for a better view. The senators were motionless, silent, and all seemed to have their eyes closed. When the silence went on for more than a minute, Matias whispered to Raisa, "What's going on?"

"They're searching for a true point," she whispered.

"A true point about what?"

"About the provision."

The moderator rang the bell. "Let's continue."

Several senators raised their hands. The moderator pointed to one, a white-haired man standing with the help of a cane.

"I felt no true point and I support the measure."

The moderator pointed to a woman nearby.

"Similar to my great friend, Mr. Jessup, I felt no true point, but I do not support the measure."

"Being that there is evidence of a lack of a true point, without any objections, I call the roll."

The moderator picked up a list and began reading out the names of individual senators and recording their votes.

Raisa rose to leave, pulling on her coat. "The voting will take quite a while. I just wanted you to see how the Senate works. I've got to get to my class."

As they walked out, Matias touched her arm. "I hope you're going to tell me what happened?"

"It was a typical vote on a provision."

Downstairs again, in the building's crowded vestibule, as she walked toward the exit doors, he touched her arm again. "You have to tell me more than that."

She stopped and looked for open seats on the wooden benches that encircled the room along the wall. She pointed to a bench that had just been vacated. They both sat.

"The first thing they did is feel for a true point on the issue," she said as she removed her coat.

"Yes, but only two of them said what they felt.

That's out of, I would guess, more than thirty senators. What about the others?"

"The fact that two didn't feel a true point meant it was unlikely any of the others would feel it either."

"Why is that?"

"Usually, all feel the same true point or none do."

"The same true point? Can't they feel different true points, some for the provision and some against? And can't some feel a true point and some not?"

She sighed. To Matias, it was the sigh of a parent whose child had asked one too many times for an explanation of something obvious.

"When certain issues come up, the senators almost always feel the same true point," Raisa said. "That's common in situations when many people have to make a decision that affects all of them, not just in the Senate but anywhere. Life is asking all of us to go in a certain direction together."

"Life is asking? I don't understand that at all."

She looked away, as if preparing a proper

response. People streamed in and out the front door on the way to and from the various Senate offices. She turned on the bench to face him directly. "How do you think of what goes on inside yourself, in your feelings? Where do you think that all originates?"

"Where does it originate? In the brain, the human brain, just as it does in you," he said.

"Talking to you, I get the feeling you believe people share a physical reality but that's all, that a person's spiritual reality is entirely their own and unconnected to anyone else's."

"Their spiritual reality?"

"The world inside them. Their feelings, everything they experience when they close their eyes. Do you believe that's your own world and no one else's?"

"I ... I ... of course I do. Your brain is separate from anyone else's brain, so yes, what your brain produces in you is distinct to you."

"So feelings are just chemical reactions or brain functions going on inside a person, and they have no connection to what's going on inside anyone else around them."

"I suppose so. Yes."

"We don't believe that. We believe people share a physical reality but also a spiritual reality. What's inside is a shared world, a shared reality."

"How can it be shared? We're physically separated."

"Spiritual reality isn't physical."

"But ultimately it's a physical world. Everything comes down to the physical."

"As I said, we don't believe that."

Matias shook his head and looked away, confounded by this but also dismissive of it, something he realized Raisa saw in his expression.

"Here's more of what we believe," she said in a challenging way. "We believe a single spirit joins us all, issuing feelings of guidance to people as they navigate the world, offering us true points. The spirit of life. It's also the spirit inside the monarchs urging them to fly south in the fall and guiding them along the way. And it's the spirit inside birds, urging them to mate and directing them how to go about it. A single unifying spirit."

"So you're saying the self I sense when I close my eyes is not really my self. It's this spirit."

"No. It's you, but it's something more too, the original life force, life itself. And it's the same life force as in everyone else too, the same life force as in all living things, the butterflies, the birds. We're all part of it, our individual souls are all mixed in with it. It joins us all."

"And if this spirit tells me to jump off a cliff, then I'm supposed to jump off a cliff?"

Her mouth tightened in anger. "That's ridiculous and you know it. Of course not. You always have to use your common sense, your good judgment. A true point is a suggestion, sometimes a very strong suggestion, but it's still your job to decide if you're going to follow it or not. There are times when life will test you with a true point that goes against common sense. The test is to see if you've wisely retained your personal judgment."

Sensing her growing irritation, he tried to gauge what to say next. He chose to be blunt. "That's quite a set of beliefs. But to me, they sound like religious beliefs—matters of faith, not of fact or science."

"Religious? What does that word mean?"

"You don't have that word? Religious?"

"No. What is it?"

Matias realized that at no time since he'd been onplanet had he heard the words "religion" or "god."

He explained what religions were, how they were typically structured and how there were followers of many versions in the colonies—Catholics, Muslims, Sikhs, Cinquists, Buddhists, Jews, Gaiaists, Mormons.

"And that's just a partial list," he said.

"Then we're not a religion," Raisa said. "At least not according to what you just said. We have no ... what did you call them? Holy books? We have nothing like that and no holy buildings or holy men or holy women. Just the opposite. We tell children not to blindly trust the advice of books, any books, or of other people, any people. What they feel inside themselves is what they should trust first and foremost. And we don't invent rules that you must live by or be judged a terrible, terrible person. For rules of living, for what someone can and can't do legally in life, we have our *Code of Colony Law*. It covers crimes, civil disputes, municipal regulations, things like that. That's the only set of rules they need to follow."

"Your beliefs are ... different. I'll give you that." He fought to stay diplomatic. "I don't really know what to say. I think ... I think your intentions are good and one can't go too far wrong doing the things one feels are right, but to explain life this way, I ..." His voice trailed off.

"You what?"

"For me, it's very hard to accept."

"We accept it," she said as she rose to leave. "No one is asking you to."

She put on her coat again, but then paused.

"Just to make it more difficult for you ... we believe something else. To be honest, this is less a belief than a best guess. But it's this. We think spiritual reality came first, that physical reality is the solid part of spiritual reality, that life created it to give consequence, for lack of a better word, to the decisions souls made. It was also life's way of giving sensual pleasure to the things souls do. Sight. Sound. Taste. Smell. Touch. They make existence a more vivid experience. One more thing we believe: The soul is eternal. It moves from one life to the next, taking the lessons of each life with it. So if you're going to doubt our beliefs, you might as well doubt all of them."

With that, she left.

That afternoon, he returned to the library and looked again at the original dictionary written for the children. Searching through it, he found no entries for "religion" or "god." No mention of "church," "lord," "deity," "creed," "synagogue," "mosque" or "bible."

He realized the original adults had deliberately left these words out. They clearly intended to give the children the chance to create a world free of established religious dogma.

The only listing in the dictionary he found that might relate to religion was this.

Faith—noun—(fay-TH) – A confidence or trust in someone or something

The Galapagos Colony

Matias felt that to spend any more time with Raisa was to invite more arguments. Now that they both knew how much of a gap existed between their beliefs, disagreements would be inevitable.

That night in his hotel, as he thought about their conversations through the day, he decided her beliefs, ultimately, were arrogant. To describe them as facts, not articles of faith, as if they could be proved with scientific experiments, was sheer hubris. Yet, the entire colony seemed to have accepted those beliefs with no reservations. Souls living in a shared spiritual reality. One inner spirit issuing guidance to all. What was her last claim? Physical reality was just a later addition to spiritual reality? It was all wishful thinking. It sounded to him like the nonsense so many religions dispensed.

Science and religion. The contentious division had existed nearly forever, he realized. But he believed in facts, in physical reality, in what one could see with one's own eyes. These things were the only reliable basis for decisions. Yes, one took into account the sort of feelings she talked about, but they were only a single factor in a larger set of things to consider. To rely almost entirely on these feelings, these vague urges and emotions arising out of the unconscious—it would be like letting a five-year-old make decisions for you. It would be irresponsible at best. At worst, disastrous.

Through the evening, he felt a growing resentment of what he saw as her condescending treatment of him that day and, indirectly, of his culture, of centuries of careful science.

All this from someone who lived in a society that traveled by horse and lit homes with candles and oil lanterns.

The next morning, he asked the governor to allow him to wander about the colony unaccompanied for the day.

He rented a horse and carriage and took the West Road toward the outlying homesteads. As he traveled beyond the village, the mix of offices, stores and residences along the roadside gradual-

ly thinned, and stands of maples, oaks, cedars and pines replaced them. The early morning's light rain had ended and sunshine appeared. He took in the rich, healthy smell of the rain-soaked fallen leaves of autumn that were collecting on the shoulder.

JPM-413, as a name, did not do the scenery justice. What had the colonists named this planet? Arcadia?

Gradually, he forgot about his disagreements with Raisa and only experienced the sensual pleasure of the drive.

It was odd. With all the species of plants and animals introduced by the settlers, for better or worse many of the colonies were not so much new worlds as they were franchises of Earth. Nevertheless, this particular landscape overwhelmed him. The hooves of the horse clipped and clopped on the packed gravel roadway and jays and chickadees chirped as they flitted through the trees beside the road.

A thought that had recurred in him often since he landed did so again: This world was stunning in its beauty.

Despite his attempts to deny it, the idea of staying continued to press at him. And a moment like this made it no easier to bury the desire.

He planned to spend a night in the shuttlebear to consult with the geologist, Corcoran, who had remained in orbit, surveying the planet with a specially fitted eyedrop capable of digging, boring and assaying.

After docking with the bear and disembarking, Matias located Corcoran as he was about to go into his sleep chamber and asked the geologist what he had found.

"Mainly that this is a fabulously rich planet

with huge deposits of precious metals—platinum, iridium, gold, rhodium. They have no idea what they have here. They use pulverized platinum for gravel in the streets, platinum that's worth a fortune."

"What about the planet itself? Why is there such a lack of animal life?"

"They had animals—huge, strange land animals. I found the calcified bones. But an extinction event occurred about 30,000 years ago. My guess is a massive asteroid hit the planet and put a cloud of dust into the atmosphere. Within a year, virtually every land animal was dead, including birds—and yes, they had birds. Only small, rodent-like creatures seemed to survive and evolution hasn't taken them far beyond that yet. That's why the species the settlers introduced—Earth's plants and animals—have done so well. There's nothing to crowd them out. Let me tell you. Mining companies will love this planet. What a feast for them."

"The colony governor might have other ideas about that."

"He can't stop them. Look what I found in the data archives."

Corcoran drew out his sightpad, called up a document and handed the device to Matias. "The original settlement ship contract. A consortium of businesses funded the *Empress of Sweden* in return for all future mining rights."

Matias recognized the contract from the library fragment. "Where onplanet are the richest deposits?"

"Everywhere," Corcoran said.

"There are two continents, though. Can't the mining companies leave the one that holds the colony alone? Maybe mine only the other one."

"Why would they? They own the mining rights to everything," Corcoran said. "This colony wouldn't exist if these companies hadn't paid these settlers' way here. They can dig wherever they want. And they will, I guarantee it. Look, I've got to sleep. I'll see you next time you're up."

Late that night in his chamber, Matias lay in bed thinking about the hard drives recovered

The Galapagos Colony

from the *Empress* by the pre-contact team. He was curious about something. True point. Were there any audio records on the drives in which the phrase was spoken by the original adults?

In the shuttlebear's cramped archives room, he isolated all the audio files on the drives. Sorting through the list, he found a cache of recordings in a subfolder labeled "history." As he listened to one of them, he realized they were continuous recordings made by the last survivors, apparently using wiffle mics that were pinned to their collars and turned on at all times. Thousands of hours of recordings.

He did an aural search to find any that included the words "true" and "point" spoken closer than twenty seconds apart.

Six results were displayed.

```
WOMAN'S VOICE (25-F-45): If what
he says is true, if you know for
sure, then, okay, what's the point
of arguing?
    MAN'S VOICE (134-M-29): Don't
point, Keisha. True, it's not his
turn, but just say that. Say it's
```

The Galapagos Colony

```
my turn.  Don't accuse someone of
(UNINTELLIGIBLE).
    WOMAN'S VOICE (76-F-21): True.
That's a good point. I hadn't, uh,
I never thought of that.
```

When he read the fourth, a shiver went through him.

```
    MAN'S VOICE (313-M-31): It's the
point of true certainty.
```

He instructed the archive screen to display all lines within thirty seconds in either direction of that particular line. The screen rapidly reset with new text. A man apparently named Mr. Hall was speaking to one or more children (only one spoke, a boy).

```
    MAN'S VOICE (313-M-31): Yes, when
you know it, when you're sure.
    CHILD'S VOICE (91-M-4): Mr. Hall,
can you say that again?
    MAN'S VOICE (313-M-31): It's the
point ... Is one of you writing
this down?
    CHILD'S VOICE (91-M-4): Duncan
is. Can you go slower? He writes
slow.
```

The Galapagos Colony

> MAN'S VOICE (313-M-31): It's the point of true certainty. The moment you feel your, uh, that you, that you feel certain you have a plan for doing something so that it will turn out ... (UNINTELLIGIBLE) ... the point you feel your plan for something will work. When you reach that point.
> CHILD'S VOICE (91-M-4): Can you spell certainty?
> MAN'S VOICE (313-M-31): Break it down into syllables.
> CHILD'S VOICE (91-M-4): A syllable is what again?
> MAN'S VOICE (313-M-31): Come on. You know what a syllable is.
> CHILD'S VOICE (91-M-4): You called it ... a true point?
> MAN'S VOICE (313-M-31): Yes. Of certainty. C-E-R. Now you try to sound out the rest.

Matias backtracked to where that thread of the conversation began. Mr. Hall was telling a group of children how to let instincts guide them when they attempted to do something they had not done before and had no instructions for doing. Parts of what he said were unintelligible as the mic apparently chafed on his collar, perhaps as he turned his head to look at one child then another.

After the portion originally displayed, the conversation became a spelling lesson. "True point" was not mentioned again over the next ten minutes of the recording or anywhere else in any of the recordings.

Matias almost laughed out loud. Their revered philosophy may have begun as nothing more than a misheard statement. A simple misunderstanding.

He transferred the trimmed audio file to his Hamblin. He would enjoy playing it for Raisa. He could imagine the look on her face as she listened. Nothing but a simple misunderstanding.

Matias returned to the colony before dawn the next morning. At his hotel, he was handed a message by the desk clerk. The governor wanted to meet at the *Empress of Sweden* that afternoon.

When he arrived, nearly all of the group that had originally gathered days earlier, including Raisa, were in the navigation room.

The governor handed him back the sightpad. "We've read through this. We—all of us—are concerned. We're not sure that we want to be part of your culture."

"I think you'd have to actually be part of it for a while to make that decision. You may benefit from being exposed to new ideas, to new perspectives," Matias said.

"I don't think so. What we read on your pad makes us very ..." The governor searched for the proper word.

Raisa provided it for him. "Worried."

"Yes," the governor said. "We don't feel your culture, the culture represented in this history you gave us, is something we can admire."

"Sir, our science—"

"Yes, your science has progressed well beyond ours. But our culture, our philosophy is—"

"If you're going to say it's superior to ours, I would strongly disagree." Matias reached for his Hamblin to play the audio clip from the archives. "Sir, I found something last night that I want you to hear. A recording."

His hand was in his carryall when he realized he had left his Hamblin in the cub. "I ... I guess I don't have it. But ... well, the point I wanted to make ..." Then he remembered he had printed out the contract and stashed it in his carryall. He drew it out. "To be honest, I don't think there is a decision. I found the original contract signed by the entire population of the *Empress*, all the original adults." He handed the papers to the governor. "The voyage that brought your ancestors here was funded by companies desiring the mineral rights."

As the governor read it, Matias explained the contract and the obligations the colony inherited.

"Many of those companies still exist and once they know that a colony flourished here, they'll want to claim their rights," Matias said. "So, you see? Legally—and I know you respect the law—legally they have the right to come. There's also a clause in the contract allowing other settlement ships to follow if the colony proved it can be viable."

He waited for the governor to finish reading.

"I don't think you have a choice," Matias said. "Others will be coming."

"Are you sure there's nothing you can do to stop them?" the governor asked.

"I can't, no. Your culture will be exposed to other cultures. You'll have to adjust to that."

After handing the papers to Raisa, the governor closed his eyes. "Yes, we respect legal contracts," he finally said. "I guess we have to respect this one."

"Unfortunately, you do." Matias said, attempting to look genuinely sad, genuinely sympathetic. But he felt neither. To call the accomplishments of his world inferior was still irritating him.

"I know Raisa asked you about this," the governor said. "But could you possibly stay behind? We all agree you'd be extremely valuable here, especially with your knowledge of science."

"I can't. I'm sorry, but I have obligations at home."

The governor looked at the others then at Matias again. "Are you sure? Don't you feel ... something that counsels you to stay?"

The question annoyed Matias. How dare they presume to tell him what he felt. "No. I have to go home."

The governor sighed and looked at the others. "Whatever happens, I suppose we'll survive and our way of thinking will survive. We'll find a way."

———

Returning to the shuttlebear that evening for the trip home, Matias realized that, in fact, there was a way to stop future ships from coming. He was the only one who knew the illness had started on the *Empress* with the tainted food supply, that it did not originate onplanet. He had never told Corcoran about the doctor's diary and he still had the stamp drive that contained it. He could tell Corcoran that he had worn his respirator the entire time he was on the surface out of fear the transmission agent still existed and that he had not been able to identify it while there. He could say in his report that the planet was not known to be safe and only native-born populations had proven themselves to be immune. Therefore, JPM-413 should be designated off limits.

As the cub approached the bear's docking arms, he debated what to do. He thought about his obligation to the companies that funded the *Empress*, companies that also helped fund JSA and his work. But he also thought about the colony, its beauty and isolation. Perhaps it was better left in isolation. Let it stay a social experiment in a unique but peculiar philosophy.

After docking, he saw through the entry room glass that Corcoran was waiting for him. What should he say?

"Ready to leave?" Corcoran asked as he secured the cub and Matias stepped out.

"I'm ready."

"Should I transmit the final report back to JSA? You have to sign off on it first. They'll want to start notifying the companies about the mineral assays I did."

Corcoran, who was tightening the restraining cables, looked up when he did not immediately get an answer. "Matias?"

"Just a second. I'm thinking." The governor's comment was running through his thoughts. "Your culture is not something we can admire."

"Yes, send it," Matias finally said. "As you say, it's a rich planet. People have a right to know. I don't have anything to add, so, yes, go ahead and transmit it."

The Galapagos Colony

THIRTY-SEVEN YEARS LATER

SYLVAN SPACE CENTER
Joint Space Administration
C Complex
Johan Wenders Avenue
Mendel Colony, 133-49L-12

DATE: 13/17/2512
TO: JSA/SDA/M. Silva
FROM: JSA/SD/Cormin White, Director
SUBJECT: Notice of Denial

   I'm sorry to say your request to delay your retirement to be part of the follow-up assessment study of JPM-413 has been denied. Because of space limitations on the shuttlebear, only one SDA officer is allowed to make the trip and we feel it would be better for a younger officer to take the position.

This will be the first official visit to the planet since your initial contact in 2475. For that reason, it would have been appropriate for you to be part of the team. I appreciate how hard you advocated to be included. However, in checking your health profile, we were concerned about your recent cardiac stress test results and also your declining motion, vision and hearing functions as you've aged. A trip of that length and the necessary confinement made us concerned about your ability to tolerate its rigors.

Again, I'm very sorry. Please be satisfied that it is your paper that resulted from the initial visit those many years ago that will form the basis for this follow-up study.

Personally, I would never put off retirement for any reason. The opportunity to enjoy the life left to me would be my priority. I imagine there will be a retirement celebration in two months when you are scheduled to leave, and I plan to be there.

Congratulations on such a long and fruitful career in the division.

The Galapagos Colony

```
Sincerely,
Cormin White, Dir.
```

Matias went anyway. He found passage on a cargo ship that left eight days after receiving the division's Notice of Denial. He used his remaining sick leave to retire early and nearly a quarter of his life savings to purchase the ticket. With no direct flight available, he had to book two connecting flights to other colonies before the final leg to Arcadia.

In recent years, he had thought often about his short time on the planet. His own colony had become unrecognizable as the settlement ships arrived in ever greater numbers. Villages had become cities, and those cities sprawled over the landscape, one blending into the next. There was no more town and country. There was only city and city. And because of the uncontrolled growth, crime had worsened, as had corruption and the inability of police and government to adequately contain either. It had become a fact of life that one lived with as best one could.

So, when he would think of the colony on

Arcadia, of its peaceful way of life, he would experience a wistful longing to return. It had become his personal vision of heaven. He was surprised at how distinctly he could remember the afternoon he rented a carriage to drive into the countryside, vividly recalling the pleasant breeze, the fresh, healthy smells in the air, the striking scenery. There were times the memory brought tears to his eyes.

Matias knew his desire to return was, in part, because of the disappointment with his life after coming home. Very little had turned out as he thought it would. He considered his life to have been two separate lives—the life that led up to the visit to Arcadia and the life following his return.

His first life had been one of anticipation. After he finished university and began his career at JSA, he felt his training and work were leading to something important. One can feel that—an expectation of great things in the future without knowing what that future will be. But the expectation is no less real.

His second life was one he thought of now as

gray years. An unhappy first marriage and divorce, an unhappy second marriage and divorce, a daughter from whom he was estranged, his lack of advancement in the space agency, and more recently the health problems common to aging.

His memories of his brief time on Arcadia had become more important to him as he aged.

There was something else about Arcadia that slowly overtook his thinking: the colony's philosophy. The deterioration of his marriages and his disillusionment with his job had changed him. He gradually lost certainty in his life and gained doubt, a healthy doubt—about himself, his life and his beliefs. As the years passed, he found he could no longer dismiss the colony's philosophy. Just the opposite. Once consciously aware of the feelings of right and wrong in himself, it was impossible to ignore them.

Later in his life, when his doubts about his way of thinking had begun to overwhelm him, when he was becoming desperate for guidance in his life, he increasingly paid attention to those deeper feelings as he made decisions, even small, seemingly trivial ones. If he felt any semblance of a "true point," of a certainty in those feelings, he was inclined to follow it.

As a result, his feelings about Raisa evolved through the years. After returning to the Mendel Colony, he viewed her as self-righteous, misguided, and, yes, arrogant. But as his own beliefs moved closer to hers, his admiration for her only grew. Indeed, she had not let this stranger from a more advanced society intimidate her. Instead, she was unwavering in her beliefs, assertively defending them and just as assertively pointing out the perceived faults in his.

Whenever he thought about their disagreement in the Senate's vestibule that last afternoon together, Matias would smile. The fierceness in her voice that day, the sharpness in her eyes, the beautiful intensity in her face. He came to realize she was possibly the most principled woman he had ever met, certainly the most admirable.

There was a moment when Arcadia's philosophy finally won a permanent place in his thinking.

A few forests beyond his colony had been permanently protected as government parks to keep them natural. On some mornings in the spring, he would drive out to one of these on his day off, park along a road and spend the day hiking back into the woods on cleared paths.

One day, with dusk approaching, he was returning to his car when he saw a pair of beavers building a dam across a slow-moving stream. He sat on a rock and watched them for nearly an hour until it became too dark to follow their movements in the water. In a shallow area of the stream, they had dragged logs and larger branches to begin the superstructure. They spent the hour bringing small rocks, grass, leaves, clumps of plants and

more mud to fill the holes in the dam.

Matias watched them with fascination. How could they possibly know how to do build such a sophisticated structure? Genes? Did he really believe that? Chemicals interacting within cells? He thought of Raisa's explanation—an aspect of life inside us all, in our souls, human and animal alike, giving suggestions in the form of feelings and instincts to those willing to pay attention.

As he watched the beavers, intent on their work, he could think of no reason to deny Raisa's words any longer.

Eight months later, with the sun just rising above the horizon, he descended slowly to Arcadia's central spaceport. It had been built to the south of the capital village, which he barely recognized. It was now a bustling city and the original wagon wheel design had been lost in seemingly random additions as the settlement expanded in all directions. He did spot the silver dome of the capitol building at its center and the grass terrace before it. However, the capitol was

The Galapagos Colony

now dwarfed by a dozen taller buildings in the city. And the gravel roads and dirt paths had all been replaced by Forgran paving. There were holographic signs and billboards throughout the city and hovers moving in all directions above it.

Once through medical screening and customs at the spaceport, Matias found a hotel nearby, surprisingly a Martin and Martin, a chain found throughout the settlement planets. Signing in at the front desk, he saw advertisements on the wall behind the clerk for a dozen other chains he recognized—restaurants, clothing stores, tech stores, even a Chastin's Casino.

His room upstairs looked identical to the room in the Martin and Martin at his planet's spaceport that he had occupied the night before he left. The coffeemaker, the VR console, the StayClean closet, the gray textured walls. He found the uniformity disturbing.

Once settled in the room, he planned to go to the library for research but was told at the front desk that the central colony library had been demolished. The printed books had been moved to a museum and all books and records were now online. It appeared the colony was as modern as the one he left.

Using one of the hotel's public computers, he searched for Raisa Olenev. He quickly found her website. She was the former chair and now professor emeritus in the Department of Arcadian History at Gateway University, which, by its address, he took to be the colony's original university. Her bio said she had served three terms in the Senate representing the 7th District, and she was married to Warren Jenson, a vice president of Jenson Technology, a company that had branches throughout the settlement colonies.

Matias seemed to remember that her husband's name was James or John and that he was also a history professor. Had they divorced?

By calling the university from his hotel room and explaining his story to the assistant in Raisa's department, he was able to get a system cell number for the Olenev-Jensens. He hung up and dialed, his heart pounding with anticipation.

"Hello?" It was a young girl's voice.

"Sorry to bother you. Is this the residence of Raisa Olenev?"

"This is her granddaughter. You want to talk to her?"

"Please."

He saw the red light come on as he was put on hold. A few seconds later, it turned green again.

"Hello?"

"Hi. I don't know if you remember me. My name is Matias Silva. I—"

"Of course I remember you."

She invited him to dinner that evening. Toward dusk, Matias took an electrocab instead of a hover to her house twenty kilometers outside the city. He wanted to see the countryside from the ground. Settling in for the ride, he realized it was the same make of electrocab, a Holden, that was most common on his planet. The familiar clear, clipped voice of the cab as it asked him for an address confirmed it.

It was fall and it had rained that afternoon. Once past the city, instead of forests and country-

The Galapagos Colony

side, he encountered unbroken stretches of residential housing and shopping centers. Trees were infrequent along the roadside. Matias opened his window, hoping that the few autumn leaves that had collected by the road would produce the same rich aroma he recalled from his carriage ride nearly four decades earlier, a scent that was essential to his memory of the planet. They did not. The air smelled more industrial than rural, more reality than dream.

Eventually, the cab came to a gravel driveway and a locked gate that opened automatically as it approached. The vehicle climbed the long, winding drive, but even before it reached the top, Matias could see Raisa standing on the home's front steps, waving as he neared.

His heart sank. Despite the conscious knowledge that decades had elapsed, he had continued to envision her as the young woman he had spent an afternoon with all those years ago, with the same youth, the same fine features and auburn hair.

In the cab's headlights, he saw she was now as

gray as he was. As he got out and went to shake her hand, he could tell by the hesitance in her eyes that she was dealing with the same shock of time's passage as he was.

"Well, aren't we the two old birds," she said.

He had to laugh. At least, her voice and smile had not changed.

"Dinner's going to be delayed," she said as they went inside. "My husband is picking up the grandkids from a party, and the children's parents are off on a walk. But this will give us a chance to talk. Would you like a drink? Some wine?"

"Please."

She poured two glasses of a Cabernet and they sat in the living room. The decor could have looked techno but it was saved by the personal touches—the framed family pictures, the pottery, the fresh flowers, the oil paintings on the walls, and most importantly, the lack of any visible electronics that were placed around a room almost boastfully in so many homes.

"Well, where to begin," she said. "So many years. First, tell me what's happened to you? A marriage? Your job?"

"Yes, two marriages, but to be honest, both my marriages and my career were less satisfying than I hoped they would be. I guess we hope for the best but have to learn to be satisfied with less."

"I'm not sure that's anything you ever learn. Your second wife didn't come with you?"

"That marriage ended in divorce also, I'm sorry to say." He tried to change the subject. "The colony ... as we were coming in, I was struck by how much it's changed."

"That's our main issue these days. Change. It hasn't been welcome. At least not by the originals. By the way, that's what anyone native has become. The originals." Her expression seemed to harden. "Within a year after you left, the new settlers began arriving, bringing with them, well, all their problems. They were very different people."

"I'm sorry to hear that."

"They looked on us, to be blunt, as simple-minded and naive."

"That's impossible. If anything, you're a very complex people, very intelligent."

"It was our philosophy they didn't like. They brought their own religions with them, and what we believed, the reliance solely on oneself, on one's feelings and little else—they had problems with that right away. Mandatory first school ended quickly. So many of the outsiders seemed to resent what we were teaching. We finally realized that many of the outsiders who were parents didn't really want their children to be self-reliant."

"How could they possibly object to that?"

"Whether they said so or not, my guess is they wanted to make some of the choices for their children. I know many discouraged them from certain marriages and careers."

"Parents have always done that."

"And in the new churches and kantons and mosques, religious leaders were angry we were teaching children to defy and ignore them. They were especially angry that we were teaching them not to take the word of any holy book over their own feelings of right and wrong. Self-reliance was not something they wanted in their followers, although they would never admit it. They would lose power if they let that happen."

"I want to confess something," Matias said. "After all these years, my thinking has moved much closer to yours. I—"

They both glanced toward the front door at the sound of a vehicle reaching the top of the gravel drive.

"My husband is back with the grandchildren," Raisa said. "Just to let you know, my first husband died of cancer just a year after you were here."

"I'm so sorry."

"I eventually remarried, but my second husband is not an original. However, he's very sympathetic to what I believe. Could we please not talk about this at dinner, though? My daughters' husbands, who aren't originals either, will also be here, and I've learned to avoid this as a subject."

Matias nodded. "I promise."

"Why don't we do this. One morning a week I volunteer at one of the last first schools still in the city, not far from your hotel. Why don't you meet me there at noon tomorrow? Before you leave tonight, I'll write down the address."

They both rose from their chairs as the front door swung open.

Some of the protesters carried hand-printed signs bearing slogans. "GOD forsakes those who forsake HIM." "Anti-religion is Pro-evil." "FIRST SCHOOLS brainwash children."

As Matias got out of the electrocab, he tried to determine if the crowd of perhaps twenty was going to threaten him if he tried to enter the school. They shouted at a woman and child who came out of the front door as they rushed through the crowd, huddling together for safety. But no one touched them.

He approached the front gate as if he were

about to walk right by, but then turned sharply and hurried by them before they could react.

"Hey, where are you going?"

He kept moving. Raisa was in the front hallway, waiting for him.

"I forgot to warn you about the protesters," she said. "Every morning for the past year, they've been out there."

"Who are they?"

"They're sent by their religious leaders. I'm not sure they even understand what we teach. But they're so loyal to their religions that they do as they're told. I don't think they're dangerous. If you stop to talk to them, they don't threaten you. They try to convert you. They know the first schools are dying out, so the violence against us has died out too."

"Violence?"

"Let's go in here." She gestured to an empty classroom.

They sat in student chairs and she told him the history of the movement against them. It began, she said, soon after the arrival of first settlement ships.

"Missionaries from a half dozen different religions came too, competing to convert us. When they realized we wanted no part of any religion, that we were specifically against that kind of influence in our lives, they grew angry. More ships arrived and the movement against us became more threatening. When two first schools were burned to the ground on the same day, fearful parents began withdrawing their children. This school has only eighteen students. Eventually, it will close too."

Raisa walked to the window to gaze at the protesters. "They aren't bad people. We bring them sanvo to drink on cold days."

"Couldn't parents, the parents who were originals, couldn't they just teach these things at home?"

"We tried that, but once the new settlers got here, many of our children were drawn away by the attraction of the things the outsiders brought with them, all the new inventions and entertainments. And when our children mixed with theirs, they picked up the outsiders' attitudes and behaviors. Our way of life was overwhelmed. Even some of our own children thought we were foolish."

"What's happened to it?"

"You mean what's happened to our way of life? I have to be honest. The way of life you remember is dead."

"Dead?"

"The people who believe this philosophy don't talk about it in public anymore. It's too controversial. But they still live the philosophy every day. Our world has come to exist only in the shadows. It's unspeakably sad."

"What about your children?"

"Some believe. Some don't. The same with the outsiders. Some came to this planet living as if they believed it although they had no name for their beliefs. They followed their feelings, their instincts, their true points, and they didn't trust much else. When we meet an outsider who believes what we do, we see it in their eyes. They're the same as us, but they don't know it.

However, most of the outsiders don't follow their feelings. They're as far from their common sense, their conscience, their true points as a person can be. So many are—and excuse me if this goes too far—but so many are selfish, greedy, corrupt, insensitive to others; all the worst qualities you can imagine."

"You know, other than from you, I haven't heard the phrase 'true point' spoken once since I've been back."

"And you won't ever hear it. It only seems to arouse anger. I try never to use it anymore." A long silence followed as Raisa watched the protesters. "Oddly, though, the way everything has turned out may be better."

"Better?"

"Sooner or later, everyone reads or hears what the originals believed. Many books have been written about it. This way, with no first school, living in a culture in which many preach against what we believe, people—even our own children—have to decide for themselves if our way of thinking has any place in their life. It becomes a personal decision, not a decision the culture makes for them."

"How is that better, though?"

Raisa turned toward Matias. "Maybe that's the way life wants it. Maybe our original culture made it too easy for our children. They were given no other choices. A person needs to ... to embrace this philosophy on their own, no matter how difficult the obstacles, for it to truly become part of their character, to become permanent in their soul."

Late that night, sitting in his darkened hotel room, the neon lights from the street throwing flashes of indigo and red on the ceiling, Matias felt completely hollowed out.

He had intended to live out his life on Arcadia, despite the prospect of losing his retirement income from JSA. Now he realized Arcadia no longer existed, at least not the world he remembered. The planet was again JPM-413, one more Earth franchise. He might as well go home.

For at least a decade, the prospect of returning

to Arcadia, of melting into its culture, into the colony's simplicity and intelligence and beauty, had drawn him forward, the sole thing in his life that had given him any hope for his future.

This room, the familiar blandness of it—and what that said about what this world had become—made him despair of ever finding a shining light in his future again. How could he possibly have chosen to leave? He knew now he had missed his chance all those years ago and it would never return. If he had stayed, what might have happened with Raisa? She said her husband had died a year after he left. Had that turned out to be a lost chance as well?

What he did know was that the only shining light in his life lay in the past. And he was as much responsible for extinguishing it on this planet as anyone.

Suddenly tired, a tiredness far beyond physical fatigue, he lay back on the bed, desiring only to sleep, to be overcome with sleep, a sleep so deep it would be impossible to ever rise out of it.

– THE END –

About the author

Stan Freeman is a former journalist whose articles have appeared in more than two dozen newspapers, including the *San Francisco Chronicle, Seattle Times, New Orleans Times-Picayune, Houston Chronicle* and *St. Louis Post-Dispatch*. He spent much of his career as the science and environmental writer for the *Springfield Union-News* and *Sunday Republican* of Massachusetts.

Born in New York City, he studied engineering at Cornell University and fiction writing in the MFA program at University of Massachusetts. He's published several short stories in literary magazines and has held a fiction-writing fellowship from the Massachusetts Council on the Arts and Humanities.

His historical mystery, *The Dutton Girl*, was released by the Seattle-based publisher, Coffeetown Press, in June of 2018.

He lives in western Massachusetts.

CPSIA information can be obtained
at www.ICGtesting.com
Printed in the USA
LVHW031924040222
710073LV00005B/564